Coke Kings 5

T.J. Edwards

Lock Down Publications and Ca$h
Presents
Coke Kings 5
A Novel by *T.J. Edwards*

T.J. Edwards

Lock Down Publications
Po Box 944
Stockbridge, Ga 30281

Visit our website @
www.lockdownpublications.com

Copyright 2021 T.J. Edwards
Coke Kings 5

First Edition November 2021
Printed in the United States of America

Lock Down Publications
Like our page on Facebook: Lock Down Publications @
www.facebook.com/lockdownpublications.ldp

Book interior design by: **Shawn Walker**
Edited by: **Lashonda Johnson**

Stay Connected with Us!

Text **LOCKDOWN** to 22828 to stay up-to-date with
new releases, sneak peaks, contests and more…
Thank you.

Submission Guideline.

Submit the first three chapters of your completed manuscript to ldpsubmissions@gmail.com, subject line: Your book's title. The manuscript must be in a .doc file and sent as an attachment. Document should be in Times New Roman, double spaced and in size 12 font. Also, provide your synopsis and full contact information. If sending multiple submissions, they must each be in a separate email.

Have a story but no way to send it electronically? You can still submit to LDP/Ca$h Presents. Send in the first three chapters, written or typed, of your completed manuscript to:

LDP: Submissions Dept
Po Box 944
Stockbridge, Ga 30281

DO NOT send original manuscript. Must be a duplicate.

Provide your synopsis and a cover letter containing your full contact information.

Thanks for considering LDP and Ca$h Presents.

Dedications

This book is dedicated to my Queen Jelissa Edwards that held me down when the world turnt they back on me. Now that we up-UP I got you for life.

Also, much love to my baby brother Jeremiah Edwards aka Gotto who kept his lips tighter than virgin pussy while the rest sang like Usher. We gon get you up out of that jam, king. We need you out here. Free the god!!!

Love to the real ones, and hell to the rest!

T.J. Edwards

Chapter 1
Kingston, Jamaica

Bonkers sat in the cabana on the beach as the aqua blue ocean water crashed into the sand loudly. Beside him was Murda. Murda wore dark shades. Bonkers looked over at him and nodded. Murda nodded back and continued to scan the beach, looking for any potential threats that may have tried to blindside Bonkers or him in any way.

Bonkers yawned. "What time kid said he'd be here again?"

Murda checked the time on his phone. It read six o'clock. "He should be coming up any minute now."

As if on cue, Flocka appeared at the edge of the beach. He had two gorgeous Jamaican women with him. One was dark-skinned, and the other light-skinned and stacked. He strolled through the sand with an air of confidence. His long dreadlocks fell to his waist. The tips were golden, as if he'd dyed them. Across his face was a pair of Dior glasses with black tints. He walked into the cabana with his hand out and extended it. "Bonkers, mon, it's a pleasure."

Bonkers shook his hand, standing up. "The pleasure is all mine. It took you long enough to get here, though, didn't it?'

"When you are as deep in the game as I am, moving about the way a man wants to becomes a little more difficult. Not everybody is a fan of Flocka. May I?" he asked, waving his hand over a seat.

"Please." Bonkers sat across from him and held up a bottle of Moët. "You sipping?"

"Sure." Flocka took ahold of the bottle and poured some into the glass that Murda provided him. "Thank you." He gave the bottle back to Bonkers.

"Now that I'm here, what's on your mind, Flocka?"

"First, I must give you my sincerest condolences for the loss of Jimmy. I know that you two were close and I can only imagine what you are going through." Flocka held up his glass as the two beauties that had come along with him stood outside of the cabana on security. Each woman had an assault rifle in her hands and wouldn't hesitate to use it with a murderous intent.

"Thank you for expressing that, but I come from thick skin. Death is a part of the game, and we must move on. Why am I here?" Bonkers drank from the bottle.

"Before Jimmy was killed - and we're still investigating that whole dilemma - but before he was taken away, Jimmy was set to take over Queens on Jamaica's behalf. I have invested a total of two million plus dollars into that borough. Money that Jimmy was supposed to use to get a strong standing within New York. Before he was killed, I feel like he was making progress." Flocka smiled. His mouth was full of gold.

"Once again, why am I here? Do you think that I'm gon' pay Jimmy's debts or somethin'?" Bonkers pointed to his chest and said this as a sly joke, but Flocka didn't laugh.

"Two million dollars may not be much money in New York, but in Jamaica, it is enough to feed an entire village for a year. With the ground that Jimmy was making, I was looking forward to relocating my people to Queens, as well as using the flip of the money to strengthen my people's lives here on the island. I am a very proud man. I love my country, and I love my people. What I don't like is to be fucked over by you, or nobody else."

Bonkers adjusted himself in his seat. "It sounds to me like you making statements that you aren't too sure about. I'ma need you to clean that shit up, and quick."

Flocka laughed. Now the sun was shining directly off his gold teeth. "Bonkers, in Jamaica it is forbidden for a drug lord to trust any man outside of the island. With that being said, I want you to know that not only did I have Jimmy's home bugged and always recorded, but Yasmin's was also. I know what took place on those nights. I watched the footage over a thousand times." He drank from his glass. "You sure this is a conversation that you would like to have around your friend here?"

Bonkers felt his heart beating faster in his chest. "We came down here together. We gon' leave together. Say whatever you wanna say. I'm all ears."

"Is that right? Okay, well here goes it." Flocka downed the rest of the glass. "What was it that spurned you to kill Jimmy? Was it the fact that he was fuckin' Yasmin behind your back, or were you envious of his lifestyle?"

"Never envious. That bitch nigga crossed me and he had to pay. I don't give a fuck who anybody is. It's respect first, and that's as simple as that. Jimmy was a snake, so I put his ass under the dirt where he belonged. What, nigga, you called me down here so you can seek retribution?"

Flocka shook his head. "N'all, that's some family shit that y'all had going on. That doesn't concern me. What does concern me is the fact that my money got caught up in the crossfire. My investments, and the imminent future of my people. You gon' have to clean that up, Bonkers."

"Oh yeah? And how might you propose I do that?" Bonkers wished he was armed. He would have gunned Flocka down along with his two bodyguards that were built like strippers.

"You, Bonkers, are going to come work for me. Since you killed Jimmy, you're going to take his spot and continue the mission that I had for him. And don't get me wrong, it ain't all work. Jimmy had the time of his life. He built up his bank account very fast and was able to go places that he had never been before. He got a pretty sweet deal. That same deal I am willing to offer you - with two stipulations."

"First of all, before we even get to those stipulations, why me? Why can't you use any other nigga to step in and take over your operations out there in Queens? Especially if you're supplying everything?" Bonkers was getting angry.

"We might as well get to the stipulations first. Which are: number one, I wanna see my people heavily populating Queens, more than ever. You'll learn why later. And secondly, I want this headache, Kammron, crushed, and Harlem under my belt. And I refuse to deny myself either one of these things."

Bonkers leaned toward him. "What you got against Kammron?"

Flocka made a disgusted face. "Kammron is the number one threat to our advancement. He is cocky, arrogant. He doesn't want to sit down and have boss conversations. He's a separatist. Instead of him uniting the people on all fronts, he chooses to segregate his people of Harlem. He thinks that they are all God's gift to humankind, and he's blown up too fast. He skipped steps. Me, personally, I don't like him, that thug that he's running with, or the borough of Harlem. One of my first priorities when all of this comes into fruition will be to make all those residents pay for Kammron's transgressions. These are my terms."

"You do know that I am from Harlem, right?" Bonkers eyed Flocka closely.

"If you were from Harlem, they wouldn't do you like they've been doing you for the last year." Flocka laughed. "You get a load of this guy?" He snickered at his security women. They laughed at him, and then went back to having serious faces, on high alert.

"Fuck is you talking about? What have they been doing to me for the last year?" Bonkers was ready to snap out.

Flocka shook his head. "You can't be this dumb." He looked Bonkers over. "Oh, you really don't know, do you?"

Bonkers shook his head. "What am I missing?"

Flocka scooted forward until he was as close to Bonkers as he possibly could be. "Kammron, Duke Da God, and Harlem have been targeting you ever since you took the throne of Queens. They've been sending jack boys and hit squads to demolish your operations. Kammron is directly connected to the former Agent Bishop of the Federal Bureau of Investigations. He has had a hand in more than a few of your people being indicted and hung out to dry by the authorities. You see, Kammron is not only playing in the streets. He is also playing the snitching game. Whenever he feels that another crew is in his way, he knocks them out of the box by any means necessary. You are nothin' more than filth to him. He's been picking off your second-rate cartel as if it was child's play. While you had your head up your ass, trying to seek revenge on Jimmy, Kammron was the one fucking Yasmin while you were in a coma and taking over Harlem, only to leave you behind like a peasant. There is so much that you're too stupid to catch that I now wonder if you really are fit to be the man that I use to take over Queens. This may be me making a major mistake. You see, I would do it on my own, but your government has made it perfectly clear that if I am caught so much as two feet inside of America, any official that sees me has a shoot to kill order in place. It's a long story." He smiled, his dark-skinned face lighting up.

Bonkers scrunched his face. He started to replay over all the events that had taken place within the last year. One by one, each move against him and his crew began to play out in his mind. The attacks against him were sinister in nature, cal-culated, and it seemed that his adversaries were always a step ahead of him. He felt angry. "How sure are you about all of this shit?"

Flocka smiled. "Kammron is new money, and he's been in the game only for a little while. I am a seasoned vet. You think he's the only one that can buy public officials or get access to sacred footage that is kept from the rest of the world?" He laughed out loud. "Yeah, the fuck, right. Money makes the world go round. Power is in the number behind your digital accounts. You are only as powerful as your political connec-tions. Your reach must extend beyond the shores of America, or you are nothing. I've been doing this shit twenty-five years strong, without a loss. I refuse to take one now." He scooted so close to Bonkers that his knee was touching his. "Rude boy, you grew up with Kammron. You know him better than any-body else. His habits, his ways, his thoughts, his weaknesses. You are going to at first conquer Queens, then Harlem, and then I will sit back and watch you crush Kammron. After he is crushed, you will be catapulted to the top of the game with us Rastafarians backing you one hundred percent. If ever you wanted to be your own man, now is the time."

Bonkers mugged him. "And if I decline?"

Flocka stood up and tapped him on the shoulder. "You won't. The opportunity is worth the rewards. Now come. You will stay in Jamaica for the next month. Get acquainted with our people. You will be treated like royalty. After this month, your allegiances will be to Jamaica. Kammron will be crushed. Let's go."

Bonkers sat still for only a moment, thinking about every-thing that Flocka had told him. Then he got up and followed behind Flocka and his security, with murder and revenge on his mind.

Murda walked beside him with his eyes straight forward. Both men were excited and ready for the next level of events.

T.J. Edwards

Chapter 2

Henny pulled the covers off of her and sat on the edge of the bed. She patted her head before digging her finger inside of her braids to get to the itching spot that was driving her crazy. She looked back at Kammron. He laid flat out with his eyes closed. The covers were pulled down to his waist. His heavily tattooed torso was on full display. She yawned and stretched her arms over her head.

Reyanna knocked on the door lightly, and then pushed it open. She stuck her head inside, thankful to see that Henny was already awake. "Pssst." She waved for her to come.

Henny frowned and ignored her for a moment. She looked back at Kammron and pulled the sheet over his frame. Even though she knew that Kammron was screwing Reyanna, she still didn't like for Reyanna to be able to ogle him whenever Kammron was in her presence. She was the Queen. Reyanna, was nothing more than a nobody. That's how she felt.

"Henny. Girl, come here." Reyanna waved for her to come again.

Henny got up off the bed, feeling groggy. She strolled across the room and grabbed her night coat from the back of the closet door. She put it on and met Reyanna in the hallway after she closed Kammron's master bedroom door behind her.

"Girl, why the fuck are you waking me up this early in the morning. What is the matter with you?"

Reyanna went into her pocket and pulled out two ultra-sound pictures. She smiled happily. "Look."

Henny grabbed the pictures from her and looked them over. "Whose are these?"

"Mine. I'm twelve weeks." She placed her hand on top of her belly.

"That's what's up." Henny kept looking at the pictures. She was about to give them back and then her stomach dropped. "Wait a minute. Who is the father?"

Reyanna took the pictures back. "That's the stupidest question you ever asked me. You already know who it is." She looked over Henny's shoulder. "I'm about to go and tell him right now. Man, I'm so happy." She started to walk around Henny.

Henny blocked her path and guided her down the hallway, away from Kammron's master bedroom. "Girl, are you sure? You mean to tell me that you ain't been messing with no other man other than Killa?" Henny felt like she was ready to throw up. How was Reyanna pregnant before she was? Over the last few months, she'd been doing everything in her power to get pregnant with Kammron's seed. She felt that would forever cement her within his heart.

"Girl, you already know that Kammron doesn't play. He ain't about to let us mess around with nobody outside of him. He's the only man that I have ever been with. Now excuse me. I gotta let him know what it is."

Henny pushed her back. She stuck her finger in her face. "Bitch, listen to me. You are not about to tell him you are pregnant. If you tell him, he is going to snap out. We got too much going on right now. That shit ain't happening. Kammron needs to be focused on what he got going on. Besides, I'm the Queen. That means I am in charge of all of you hoes. That includes you. Take yo' ass in your room until we can come up with a solution for this baby." She guided her toward the room that she was staying in.

Reyanna spun out of her guidance. She stopped defiantly in the middle of the hallway. "Henny, I don't know what's wrong with you, but you need to get the hell out of my way before I am forced to get on that bullshit with you. Now, I have been very patient and respectful ever since I've been living with y'all, but enough is enough. You are testing my patience."

Henny grew furious. "Aw, so you think you're all big and bad now that you're havin' Kammron's baby? Really, bitch?"

"And you mad 'cause you ain't? What's wrong with you, anyway, huh? That nigga be fuckin' you every day, bussing inside of you, and you still ain't never came up pregnant with his kid. You sure you ain't dead on the inside? Or maybe it's all of the dope that you do that's made yo' ass sterile." Reyanna stepped into her face. "I've watched so many movies with this whole royalty type shit and I know that a queen can't be a queen unless she is able to have a man's seed. Don't look like you gon' be able to do that no time soon - or at least not before me. Therefore, I got a chance to bump you out of yo' slot. But don't worry, I ain't gon' treat you half as bad as you treated me while I was the low woman on the totem pole." Reyanna got so close that her forehead rested up against Henny's. "Get yo' worthless ass out of my way so I can go and tell my baby daddy the good news."

Henny held her head down as all her anger, jealousy, and frustration came flowing through her all at once. She cocked back and pushed Reyanna with all her strength. Reyanna went flying backward. She wound up on her back by the entrance to the kitchen. Henny ran and jumped over her. She grabbed a steak knife out of the wooden knife holder and ran back into the hallway, where Reyanna was just getting up.

Reyanna held her rib. "You're evil, Henny. You're an evil, sadistic, bitch."

"Pack yo' shit right now and get the fuck out of my man's house. If I ever catch you sniffing around him again, or if you ever tell him about that punk-ass baby that's growing inside of you, I will kill you. I will hunt you down and make a spectacle out of taking your life. You have my word on that."

Reyanna eyed her with hatred. "You know what, Henny? You can have him because the way I see it, none of this is going to last anyway, and you most definitely need him more than I ever will. I will make my own way in life. I don't need some man, so fuck you and fuck Kammron. Both of y'all can kiss my ass."

Kammron stuck his head out of the bedroom door. "What she just say?"

Reyanna froze with her eyes bucked. "Nothing. I was just goofing off."

Kammron mugged her and then looked over at Henny. "Put that bitch in her place, then come and jump in the shower with me. I need to feel your brown skin for a minute." He slipped into the bathroom.

Henny glared at Reyanna. "Bitch, you got ten minutes to get the fuck out of here and be thankful that I ain't killing you right now."

Reyanna nodded. "Okay, Henny, you got that. Let me just get my things and I'll be on my way." Reyanna headed into her bedroom and closed the door.

As soon as the door closed, tears dropped from Henny's eyes. Her throat got tight. She wondered if there was something really wrong with her. She walked into the living room and sat on the arm of the couch with her head hung. "What the fuck is life?"

Reyanna came out of the bedroom with a .45 in her hand. She stormed into the hallway with her eyes blazing with anger. She headed to the bathroom and opened the door. Kammron was inside lathering himself up with his body wash. He heard the door open and smiled. "'Bout time yo' ass hurried up. I got some shit I gotta handle, and I need a quick shot of my baby first."

Reyanna closed her eyes and took a deep breath. "I'm tired of being your bitch, Kammron. I'm tired of you treating me like shit!" She waited for Kammron to pull back the shower curtain with a look of shock and disbelief on his face. She aimed at him and started shooting with the intent to kill.

***

There was a full moon in the sky when Bonkers pulled up in front of Kammron's mansion at eleven o'clock in the evening with fifteen cars and trucks rolling beside and behind him. Bonkers stepped out of his Range Rover dressed in black fatigues and a black ski mask. In his hand was a hundred round Draco. The Jamaicans that accompanied him wore the same attire as Bonkers. All were strapped and ready for war.

Bonkers stepped in front of Kammron's mansion with a grenade in his left hand. All of the things that Flocka had put him up on was going through his mind all at once. How could Kammron have betrayed him in such a way? How could he himself have been so stupid? The more he thought about it, the angrier he got. He took the grenade and pulled the pin out of it, tossing it as hard as he could through Kammron's front window. "It's war, bitch nigga, and there can only be one king!"

T.J. Edwards

Chapter 3
One year later...

"How does dat feel? Is good?" the 5'1" gorgeous little Asian girl asked while she meticulously rubbed her hands up and down Kammron's back. She purposely avoided his war wounds from fear that she would cause him any discomfort.

Kammron kept his face inside of the table's hole while he looked over the contents of his cell phone. "Shorty, you doing good. If you wasn't, I'da already had a few of the Coke Queens in here all over yo' ass. Just keep getting the don right and everythang will turn out just the way that it's supposed to."

She nodded. "Okay, sounds like plan."

Kammron furrowed his eyebrows as he mugged the phone's screen. "What the fuck is going on here?"

"'Cuse me, sir?" the beautiful Asian girl asked him.

"Nah, shorty, I'm talking about what the fuck I'm looking at on this screen. "Just keep doing ya thing, and don't ask me shit else unless it's really necessary. Ya understand dat?"

She nodded. "Sounds like plan." Her small hands roamed all over his back. She applied more oils and added pressure.

Kammron looked over Duke's Instagram account again. Some of the major kingpins of New York were calling Duke Da God the king of Harlem. Kammron couldn't quite put his finger on why, but the whole imagery of Duke being held in such a light and given his title was making him feel angrier than he'd ever felt in all his life. Ever since Reyanna had hit him up in the bathroom with one slug after the next, Kammron had a rough time getting back physically, and instead of being ten toes down in the field, he'd allowed for Duke Da God to walk through the trenches of Harlem and keep everything in order by his words from afar. Duke was responsible for solely keeping Harlem at the top of the food chain, and thus far he'd done every bit of that. Kammron didn't like the prestige that was coming along with his duties.

"Yeah, I don't know about this shit right here. I think it's time for me to make my presence known once again. What you thank, shorty?" He turned on to his back and situated his pink towel so that it continued to cover his lower half.

The Asian woman shrugged her shoulders. "Don't know you. Don't know what you talk 'bout. I finish front now is what you ask?"

Kammron nodded. "Hell yeah, but fuck all those other regions, ma. I need you to get the god right in this lane." He took ahold of her small hand and brought it toward his piece. The closer he got, the more she began to resist him. "Don't be scared, shorty, this is Harlem's finest right here."

"I kint do dat. Against rules. No touch dare. Put towel back on."

Kammron shook his head. He grabbed a handful of her hair and brought her face close to his after slipping a .40 Glock from under his clothes that were situated on the chair directly next to the bed. He pressed the Glock to her cheek and lowered his eyes to slits. "Say, li'l baby, do you know who the fuck I am, or has the whole world forgot? Who am I?"

"Don't know who you are, but you hurt my head. Let me go. You leave now or get trouble from poe-leese."

Kammron tightened his grip. "You threaten the god? Bitch, is you crazy?"

She yelped as his grip got tighter and tighter until she was on her knees. Kammron stood up and watched his towel drop beside the Asian beauty. He stroked his dick with one hand and with the other he brought her face closer to him. She closed her eyes and tightened her lips together.

"Look, I don't give a fuck if we gotta be here all night. Yo' li'l fine ass about to hit me off like you supposed to or I'ma holler at Poppa Kim and get that ass deported back to Korea, where you already know how they about to handle dat ass. I think it's in yo' best interest to make this happen. Open yo' ma'fuckin' mouth."

She shook her head from right to left. "Kint do dat. I'm not old enough. You get in trouble. I'm just girl."

Kammron's eyes bucked open. "A girl, yeah?" He scooped her up and slammed her on the table. He got between her shapely thighs and maneuvered himself in between them. Once there he reached under her skirt and ripped her panties from her frame. The white cotton was tossed over his shoulder before two fingers entered into her tight entrance while he sucked on her neck. She groaned and tried to push him off of her. This only excited Kammron all the more. He pulled her to him and stroked his dick for a few more seconds, then he rubbed the head up and down her crease. Her sex lips parted. He jerked his hips forward and slipped deeply into her. She gasped and smacked at his chest for the first ten strokes. Kammron grabbed her aggressively and proceeded to pounding her out with long deep strokes that forced her into a moaning submission. He roared and fucked her as hard as he could, noting how tight and wet her pink pussy was to him. Her eyes rolled into the back of her head. He placed her ankles on his shoulders and beat her walls loose with no regard. She screamed and hollered at the top of her lungs.

"Yeah, yeah, li'l bitch. I feel dat shit. I feel you squirting all over my joint. I don't care how young you is, that box was ready." He increased his speeds and juiced her box for all it was worth.

Henny heard the sounds of distress from the hallway. She dipped her hand into her Birken bag and came out of it with her trusted .380. She burst through the door and stopped in her tracks as she watched Kammron try to drill a hole through the Asian girl. His ass nearly touched his back before he dove forward with his thrusts bottoming her out. The Asian girl had managed to wrap her legs all around his torso while she took everything that was being handed down to her in both pain and oblivion. This caused Henny to become angry. She made her way to the bed to break the sexing pair apart when the Asian girl bear hugged Kammron and arched her back with her face to the ceiling. She started to shake and let out an ear-piercing scream before she came so hard that she began to shake right along with Kammron as he dumped his seed deep into her womb. The girl fell to the table and Kammron pulled his dick out of her with his pipe leaking her secretions of pleasure.

Henny wanted to kill both of them. "Kammron, what the fuck is going on?"

Kammron wiped his dick off on the pink towel and started to get dressed. "Yo, this bitch got to giving a nigga a happy ending and you already know how dat shit go. Why the fuck you making so much noise? You tryna get a nigga a case or somethin'?"

Henny mugged him, and then ventured her eyes down to the Asian girl, who lay on the table with her left hand rubbing her box. Her kitty was swollen and slightly opened. Juices trickled out of her and ran down her ass. "It's like I can't leave a room for a second without you fucking a bitch. Why are you so damn raunchy?"

"What? Man, bitch, I don't even know what the fuck that word mean. What's done is done." He pulled out a knot of hundreds and dropped them on the table beside the girl, who was breathing harder and harder every second it seemed.

Henny rubbed her temples in a circular motion. "Yeah, a'ight, Killa. Let's get the fuck out of here before yo' ass do wind up in jail. I don't think that li'l bitch is no bit of sixteen yet and if she ain't, well, I don't even wanna think about that. So let's go."

Kammron kissed the girl on top of her head. "Shid, if she ain't, she damn sho' know how to take some dick. I ain't got no complaints. Hell, if these Asian folks would, I'd take her ass home with me and keep her li'l ass confined to one of my rooms just for that thang between her thighs. Damn, that box good as a ho."

"Whatever." Henny rolled her eyes and left out of the room.

"Yo, wait up!" Kammron called.

Before he could get out of the room Poppa Kim, a short Korean man with black hair with a big bald spot in the middle of it, blocked his path. He looked past him. "Killa, what you do wit' my baby daughter who a kid? You no touch I hope."

Kammron tapped him on the shoulder. "Come on now, boss, you already know the shit that Killa won't do. Shorty all good. I ain't touch her." He looked over at her. She was embarrassed to look her father in the eyes, so she avoided them. Instead, she started to clean up the room while kicking her torn panties under the table out of sight. Kammron saw this action, laughed, and left the massage parlor after tapping Poppa Kim on the shoulder again.

When he got outside and into the Bentley truck, Henny was inside of it with an angry scowl on her face. Summer Walker played out of her speakers. She pulled her seat belt around her and revved the engine. "You ready to go?"

"Fuck wrong wit' yo' emotional ass now?"

"Don't start wit' me, Kammron, 'cause every time some bullshit happens, you always try and make it seem like there is something wrong with me when it's yo' ass. I don't understand why we can't go nowhere without you always trying to fuck a bitch. That don't make no sense to me."

"I been like this since before yo' li'l ass met me. I can't help it. I love pussy, and ain't no such thing as one pussy ever being enough for me. That's just the way that it is."

Henny shook her head again as she pulled out of the parking lot. "Do you have any idea how insulting that is to me though?"

"How insulting what is?"

"What you just said." She looked over at him and then back to the road.

"Hoes always taking about they want the truth. That they hate that lying shit. But when a nigga gives it to they ass in the raw, they don't know how to handle it. I could have easily lied to yo' ass, but n'all, I'm keeping that shit a buck in a half."

"Lucky me." She rolled her eyes again.

"Fuck is yo' problem, shorty? I really ain't understanding you right now, as hard as I'm trying to."

"Nothing, other than the fact that ever since day one I been holding yo' ass down. I make shit happen all the way from South Carolina where we are hiding out at, all the way back to New York. I make sure that shit run smoothly right alongside of Duke Da God's ass."

"Bitch, that's yo' place to do that. I put you in a position to make that shit happen like that. And Killa ain't hiding out from nobody other than the Feds - let's make that shit explicably clear."

"Whatever, nigga What I'm saying is that I deserve a little more gratitude than what you been giving me. When will you think on a settling down with just me level, or at least respect me enough to not fuck random bitches without a rubber. Ain't we trying to get pregnant?"

"That's what I thought, but it don't seem like yo' body wanna cooperate. That's the problem."

Henny mugged him with intense hatred. "Rude-ass nigga!"

"What?" Kammron didn't understand what he'd said that had been so offensive.

"Damn, Kammron, nigga, you already know how this trying to get pregnant thing is affecting me. I'm starting to feel like it ain't never gon' happen, and that's tearing me up inside. The fact that you could blurt out something so callous speaks volume to your character."

Kammron shrugged his shoulders and popped a Percocet. "I don't give a fuck what you talking 'bout. I speak the real. That's all I can do. You can't handle that shit, then that's on you. I ain't in the bidness to be with all of that emotional shit all of the time."

Henny shook her head, and took a deep breath before she looked over to him. "Damn, Kammron, so what do you see me as, huh?"

"What do you mean?"

"It's a pretty simple question. I just wanna know, what do you see when you look at me?"

Kammron pulled his nose and ran his tongue across his gums before he tooted four thick lines of heroin. He needed to get in his mode. He could tell that Henny was dead set on getting on his nerves. He waited until the music from the heroin kicked in, and then he turned towards her with a smile on his face. "I see my bitch."

She was silent for a moment. "Nigga, dat it? Just yo' bitch?"

"Fuckin' wit' a nigga like me, that's all I need to see. Fuck more you wanting me to peep?"

She waved him off and snickered. "Yeah, awright, since that's all you see, that's all I'ma be den?"

"That's all you've ever been. I don't know what the fuck you got going through yo' head, but you better straighten up and fly right real quick or you're about to be in for a rude awakening. Word up."

She nodded and kept driving. "Cool, Killa, yo' bitch heard you. I'ma do just that. You can bank on it." She slid her Cartier frames over her eyes as an array of evil thoughts entered into her mind all at once.

Chapter 4

Bonkers stepped onto the balcony of his ten room mansion and stretched his arms over his head. "Ahhhhhh!" he hollered and waited until his bones popped before he lowered them. Up ahead, the sun was just starting to peek over the horizon in an orangeish-yellowish glow. Huge seagulls flew across the air, squawking loudly. The scent of the salt of the sea wafted to him. He ran his tongue all over the Dutch Master before lighting the tip of it and puffing the flame inside of the cigar. Thick clouds of smoke rose from the Syracuse Orange strand of cannabis.

Reyanna appeared in the doorway dressed in a skimpy red and black silk negligee. She slipped her arms around his waist and laid her face on his back. "Good morning, daddy. How did you sleep?" Her belly slightly protruded due to her pregnant state, and even still, she was quite the sight for Bonkers.

Bonkers blew his smoke toward the air just as a monstrous black hawk flew past him with its long wings flapping effortlessly. "I slept good. How about you, baby girl?"

She hugged him tighter and sighed. "Amazing. It's like being up here on Staten Island has me sleeping so peacefully. I haven't been this mentally free in a long time."

"That's what sleeping with the enemy gets you." He laughed and turned around to face her. "Yo, I think I done let that nigga Duke Da God get big enough. I'm ready to crush that nigga and forever cement myself as the king of Harlem, and the best to have ever done it."

"But baby, I thought you were over the whole Harlem take over scenario."

"What the fuck would make you think something like that?" Behind him, the waves crashed into the shore and a loud horn sounded from a nearby ship.

"Because Queens is yours. Everyone knows this, and we've just locked down a deal on a shipment of narcotics that will basically hand us over the Bronx. Don't nobody care about funky-ass Harlem - at least they shouldn't."

"Hey, watch yo' mouth, ma. I know I done been locked in with these blikkas against the borough, but at the same time that's my homeland. I was born and raised in that ma'fucka, and I'ma always have Black Heaven in my heart. A ma'fucka ain't seen Kammron in over a year. I know that fool dead as a bitch. Duke Da God was adopted by Harlem. That nigga ain't bred by the blood that was shed in my borough. I don't want him being hailed as the king of shit. Besides all of that shit anyway, had me and that nigga Killa never fell out, we would have ran that bitch together as dons. But you already know what that greed and envy do to niggas every time. It is what it is, plus my li'l niggas constantly drilling Duke's niggas and vice versa. They touting Duke as king and I ain't going."

Reyanna became irritated. "I thought you always said that niggas can't war and make money at the same time."

"What the fuck that got to do with anything?" He puffed from his blunt and inhaled the smoke deeply before blowing it into her face.

"Well, I can't wrap my head around you making all of this money. You're back and forth from New York to Jamaica, eating like a glutton. Everything is falling into place for the greater good of your squad and you want to risk all of that, not to mention your new political connections, all for the sake of a dirty, rotten, filthy borough like Harlem, where the murder rate is up eighty percent, and poverty is up even higher than that. Please tell me how that makes any sense whatsoever?"

Bonkers looked her over for a moment and then turned his back on her. He looked over the large body of water that was directly in front of them. "Shorty, you used to fuck wit' Kammron the long way, am I right?"

"Yeah, and? What does that have to do with anything?"

"I ask that to say that you used to be down with that nigga on a daily. Now you fuckin' wit' me the same way, I assume."

"Bonkers, why are we discussing this right now? I'm supposed to be here and all about you. Don't forget that you courted me, and you found me after you learned that I put Kammron down. You said that I was the perfect woman for you because it takes a lot for a female to do what I did, and that some of the hardest niggas in New York didn't even have the heart to do it. Now for some reason it sort of feels like you're coming at me sideways. Why is that?"

Bonkers sucked his teeth. "If I was coming at you sideways, shorty, you'd know that shit. I just got a hard time trusting anybody. In my mind, every ma'fucka is shady and their loyalty don't last for too long. Ever since you came out here and slipped your arms around a nigga's waist you been trying to talk me out of kicking shit off with those Harlem niggas. I can't even think straight without handling my bidness. All of the money in the world ain't gon' fill the void that I feel deep inside of myself until I drill that nigga Duke and find out if Kammron's bitch ass is really dead."

"That's stupid to even wonder because I know for a fact that he is. I shot him three times. I saw the bullets go into him and drop him before that crazy bitch Henny started capping at me."

"Yeah, well, had I knew y'all had a second hideaway, I would have blew that ma'fucka up instead of the one that I did, and we wouldn't be having this conversation." Bonkers faced her. "I got a real bloodlust right now. Once you put a few niggas in that soil, that hunger for more skulls under your belt eats away at you more and more each day until it becomes a sickness - kinda like what I got right now." He rubbed the side of her face and looked into her eyes. "I'll tell you what though. After I crush these niggas in Harlem, I'll be able to move on with my life, and then it can be all about the money. I got a lot of funds tied up that's gon' produce some real residuals. I can't even begin to focus on that shit until I handle this though."

Reyanna lowered her head and shook it. "So where does that leave me, and when will you begin to trust me?"

"I don't know where that leaves you, and as far as the trust thing goes between the two of us, ma, I don't know. I don't really trust no nigga or no bitch. That's just the way it is. But I will keep you close and always place you within a position to win. You can't really ask for more than that right now because shit is real hectic." He kissed her forehead and walked into the bedroom just as the sun began to illuminate the sky outside with a reddish hue.

Reyanna followed behind him with her shoulders slumped. "I don't know what the fuck I done got myself into. Sometimes I wish I would have stayed in school and ran track. I probably would have been in the Olympics already. Don't you know that I held the record in the United States as a senior for the one and two hundred yard dash? What the hell was I thinking getting involved with a bunch of dope boys?"

Bonkers mugged her. "Shorty, I'm far from a dope boy. I got fifty dope boys working under me, and all of them niggas is seeing crazy dollars. That makes me the plug. To me the words dope boy being attached to me in any way speaking of my own hustle is a slap in the face. I been doing this shit way too long to just be a dope boy type nigga."

"But you know what I mean though, damn. I don't know what level you're on, and I ain't trying to take nothing from you. All I'm saying is that I'm rocking with you, that's all.

Now what is it that you truly want me to do to prove that shit to you?"

Bonkers flopped on the bed and pulled her down on top of him. His big hands gripped her rounded ass, squeezing it. "Whether you know it or not, I got a real special place for you on my team. Any bitch that'll drill the great Kammron deserves a spot in my kingdom, so I got'chu. But for now and until I bless you with the knowledge of what you gon' be used for, I just need you to stay in yo' lane and to keep doing the shit that you been doing, 'cause that's all that matters right now, and in due time every thang that's supposed to fall into place; will. Trust and believe that." He kissed her lips. "You got that?"

She nodded and smiled. "Yeah, daddy I got that." She kissed his lips and savored the taste of him.

There was a major difference between Kammron and Bonkers for her. Kammron was cold-hearted, callous, too outspoken, and harsh, and in the sheets he was a savage lover with no regard for the vagina other than to beat it into submission. Bonkers was outspoken, yet kind and understanding. He was thorough in everything, but distrusted everyone. His sex game was superb, but disconnecting. He gave her just enough passion to let her know that if ever she became his main that their nights alone would be promising. But it was about more than sex for Reyanna. She wanted love and she wanted the title of being the wife, as childish and unrealistic as that seemed. She felt it was possible, and she was willing to do whatever she had to in order to lock Bonkers down because she was certain that he was about to be as big as Sean Carter in New York and beyond.

Bonkers slipped his fingers into her crack from the back and slid them in and out slowly. "I like you, li'l mama. I mean, I really, really do. Just do what you been doing and let me assess you from afar and everythang is going to be awright. You got my word on that. Okay?"

Reyanna kissed his lips. "Okay, daddy, I'm 'bout dat and whatever for you then. Just give me the order and watch me carry it out. Besides, according to the streets I'm a dead woman walking anyway because I offed Kammron, so what do I really have to lose?"

Bonkers shook his head. "Sounds like you got everything to gain, ma, and so do I. Yeah, shorty, so do I." He pulled his fingers out and sucked them into his mouth as a boisterous banging sounded on the bedroom door. He pushed her off of him and slipped his hand under the bed, grabbing his F&N and cocking it. "Who the fuck is it?"

Reyanna rolled to the floor and took ahold of her black Cat .9. She cocked the hammer and ran to the side of the door with her back to it. She locked eyes with Bonkers and nodded at him while at the same time reaching for the doorknob. He winked at her. Reyanna twisted the knob and pulled the door open. Bonkers knelt to one knee, ready to shoot with no mercy. When his eyes rose and he locked vision with the target, his face became a mask of fury.

Chapter 5

Murda stepped into the doorway and held his hands up with a smug smile on his face. His eyes darted from Bonkers over to Reyanna, who was now holding two .45s in her hands with her chest heaving up and down. Murda surveyed Bonkers, who was also holding his firearm at him. "Say, Dunn, what the fuck y'all asses on? Did something happen involving the god that I don't know about?"

Bonkers grabbed him by the shirt and pulled him inside of the mansion. He stepped on to the porch and looked out into the night. His shooters patrolled the grounds, angry and alert. They saw him and they nodded at him to ensure him that everything was all good. Bonkers slipped back into the mansion and closed the door behind him.

Reyanna patted Murda down and uncovered his .44 Desert Eagle. She pulled the clip out of it and cocked the gun so that the bullet hopped out of the top of it, then she handed the gun back to Murda and walked a safe distance away, mugging him from that vantage point.

"Yo, what's with the treatment, B? Y'all acting real strange and shit." Murda said this with his arms outstretched before he tucked his gun into his belt.

Bonkers holstered his weapon and grabbed a bottle of Ducè off of the table. "Nigga, this is how I gotta roll ever since I found out that Kammron's bitch ass been on some snake shit all along."

"Yo, kid, but you already know me, and you know that I don't get down like that." Murda said this feeling offended. He side-eyed Reyanna and felt a twinge of jealousy for being allowed to be in her position instead of his own.

"Nah, son, I thought I knew Killa's ass too and that nigga turned out to be a straight fraud. I gotta run shit how I run shit from here on out. That's just the score. It ain't nothing personal, and if you fuckin' wit me this is how it's going to be. Word up." Bonkers sipped out of the bottle and looked him over closely. "Besides all that, it's too much money going around and niggas constantly switching sides left and right. Ma'fuckas always gon' be more loyal to the money than they will their homie. The game taught me that."

Murda waved him off. "Not me, nigga. I'm cut from a different cloth; always have been. I guess you'll find that shit out in due time though. In the meantime, we may have a problem."

Bonkers took a long swallow and never took his eyes off of Murda. He lowered the bottle and sat it on the table burping under his breath. "Oh yeah? And what is that?"

"That nigga Flocka been moving his troops all over Queens for the last four days. I don't know what he's preparing but it seems real fishy to me, especially since I ain't got no green light from you that any of this shit was about to take place." Murda pulled an old school Dutch Master stuffed with Kush out of his inside jacket pocket and sparked it, inhaling the smoke deeply to calm himself down.

"Ain't nobody told me nothing about no shit like this. When the fuck was you gon' tell me?" Bonkers scooted to the edge of the couch and focused intently on Murda. Outside, he could see the shadows of his men pacing back and forth on guard with assault rifles in their hands. Murda had been given clearance to step up to his door front. He was wondering if that was something that he should change considering his lack of trust factor.

"I'm telling you now, king. I had to make sure that it's what Flocka was really on. Now you know I still got my own ties back to the island, and word around Jamrock is that there is major money to be made in Queens and especially in Harlem. They say those Choo and Woo niggas already got Brooklyn going under 'cause of all the murdering and shit, so ain't nobody trying to touch Bucktown or nowhere inside that borough. The action is in Queens and Harlem. The people back home say you soft, kid. They say ain't no way you gon' be able to oust Duke and Killa, if that nigga still alive. Flocka sending troops 'cause he wanna take over ya shit all across the board. I'm just keeping that shit a buck. And since we're getting most of our guns and weaponry from that nigga, on top of most of the narcotics for the borough, what the fuck do we do?"

Bonkers was already up and hitting Flocka's phone. It rang ten straight times before it was sent to voicemail. He tried it again and again and received the same result. He tossed his phone on to the couch. It bounced off of the cushion and hit the floor, activating his Apple music app.

"Yo, all you gotta do is tell me what the deal is, Dunn. You feeling like you want the gang to go over and holler at them niggas, then say dat shit. Word up. I love the island. I bleed green and black. But that ain't what's paying me."

Bonkers stood up and pulled at the sparse hairs of his chin. His face turned into a mug of anger and frustration. "That nigga was just praising me and all of that shit. Now you saying kid sending troops over and shit like I'm about to let him just conquer my operations and all of dat? Nah, B, fuck all of that shit. I'm hopping on a flight first thing in the morning and going to check the temperature personally. I ain't never feared no nigga. Fuck he thank they call me Bonkers for?"

Murda shook his head. "Yo, I know you can hold ya own and all of that shit, but I don't think that would be smart. What type of nigga walks into his own slaughter? You at least have to give yourself a fighting chance, and travelling to Jamaica after all of the crazy shit that just took place down there kicked off is bananas. He clip you, then what the fam back home gon' do? You forget how many niggas that's eating off of yo' plate?"

Bonkers grunted. "Hell n'all I didn't. But that's why I gotta make sure that everythang is everythang because I have invested into a whole lotta of ma'fuckas and I ain't got my return just yet. Before Flocka thank he 'bout to come up to the boroughs and get stupid I gotta put an end to that shit. That's just the way it gotta be.

"I hear all of that shit right there, let's just make sure that whatever you're about to do make sense, and I think it's in your best interest to take a cruise through Queens first before you hop off of the deep end. See the shit that I am seeing, and if that calls for you to move how you thinking, then I'm behind you one hundred and ten percent," Murda assured him before taking four strong puffs off of his Dutch.

"Sounds good, B. Let's load up the Bentley and make it happen. Time is money, and we ain't got enough of either to lose a pinch of neither one."

Bonkers nodded at Reyanna and five minutes later, she was pulling the Bentley truck around to the front of the mansion and they were hopping inside of it, headed to Queens.

***

Kammron took the custom gold razor blade and chopped through the ounce of Saudi Arabian heroin that was situated before him. He made four thick lines of the product before taking a hundred dollar bill and tooting up two of the lines hard. He pinched his nostrils closed and groaned as the harsh drug took effect. As soon as he was high as gas prices, he sank back again the sofa and began to nod in and out of consciousness while licking his lips and occasionally sipping from a bottle of codeine-spiked Korbel. On the big 4K television in front of him, the news reporter spoke about a triple homicide in Brooklyn.

Kammron shook his head. "Yo, them young niggas wilding out those ways, B. Seems like ain't no more structure. But that's alright though, 'cause once they done killing each other and all of that, I'ma have my li'l niggas move in and shut that bitch down. I gotta have all of New York. The god starting to get greedy."

Henny stepped into the doorway with her hand on her waist and her head turned sideways. "Yo, Killa, who the hell are you talking to?" She saw the dope on the table and his state and grew depressed. It seemed to her like his habit was getting worse.

"Yo, when you're a god, you speak out loud and the other gods hear you. That's all I'm doing. Fuck is you ear hustling for?"

"Nigga, ain't nobody ear hustling if yo' crazy ass is talking out loud." She rolled her eyes and came further into the living room. She held a positive pregnancy stick out in front of him. "Look at this shit right here, Killa."

Kammron closed his eyes for a moment, and then slowly opened them. He tried his best to focus in on what she was holding. He closed his eyes again over it. "Fuck is you holding? You already know this shit be having my eyes fuckin' wit me."

"I'm holding ya seed, nigga, and it's about fuckin' time too. You see this? Huh?" She held it in front of his face and then tossed it on his lap.

Kammron brushed his lap off and the stick fell to the floor. He grabbed his Korbel off of the table and downed a quarter of it. "Congratulation. I know that's what you've always been hoping for."

Henny popped her head back. "Excuse me?"

Kammron went into a deep nod. He hunched over and began to snore with his mouth wide open. A minute later he sat up and wiped his lips. "But that's what's up though. I guess you think that's about to change some shit up then, huh?"

Henny could not believe what she was witnessing, nor the things that were coming out of his mouth. "Yo, Killa, I'd be lying if I didn't say you wasn't blowing me right now. You already know how I feel about you, and how much us having a baby together really means to me. Why you can't let me have this li'l bit of joy?"

Kammron stood up on wobbly legs. His old stomach wounds seemed to hurt him for a moment, and then the pain subsided. He still covered them with his left hand. He reached out for her. "Come here, goddess."

She shook her head. "N'all, nigga, answer my question."

Kammron tried once again to extend his love. "Yo, bring ya as here before I gut punch yo' simple ass, word up."

"Nigga, you gut punch me, on everythang I love, I'ma stamp ya black ass on a T-shirt for all of the niggas in Harlem to rock. I don't even know why you would say some dumb shit like that anyway."

Kammron pulled her by the arm and wrapped her into his embrace. He brought his lips down to her forehead a d held them on her skin. "Word to Jehovah, I'm beaming that you having my seed. Out of all of the bitches from the borough that could have wound up popped, I'm just glad it's you. That's real emotion right there."

She pushed him away from her. "Get off of me. You sound crazy as a Betsy bug is." She dusted her clothes off and shook her head. "You know what, Killa?" She paused and took a deep breath. "I already see that yo' ass is incapable of sharing the spotlight for even a second and allowing for somebody else other than yo' ass to be as or more happy than you are. All I wanted was this moment and on everythang, you ruined that shit."

Kammron sat on the couch and sank his head between his knees. He nodded for a moment. Sounds of the television played in the background. He opened his eyes and looked up at her. "What do you want me to do? How can I make you feel happy? I'll do anything, and you're the only bitch that'll ever hear me say some shit like that."

Henny winced at his harsh words. Sometimes the first re-action is all a woman needs to see. It tells you everything. Gon' head on with your day Kammron. It's good." She left from the room feeling both her anger and emotions well up inside of her.

"Well fuck you den! I don't know what you want from me. You hoes need to tell a nigga. Y'all too sensitive. Too quick to cry and shit. Who the fuck gon' cry fa me, huh? The shit is irritating." He downed the rest of his drink and dropped the bottle to the carpet. "How the fuck do you expect a nigga wit' twenty-one bodies under his belt to be emotional? That shit ain't real! It just ain't!" He tooted two more lines and laid back, frozen.

Henny stood in the hallway with her back up against the wall and tears running down her cheeks. She wiped them away and shook her head. "I just don't understand what more I have to do. A woman can only take so much before she cracks." She placed her hand on her stomach and tilted her head back-ward, facing the ceiling. "Father, I'm losing my strength. Please show me a sign."

T.J. Edwards

Chapter 6

"Yo, you see what the fuck I was talking about, B? This nigga Flocka got all types of dread heads posted up all through the borough. Just look at this shit." Murda said this as they turned the corner and headed down a long strip coming directly out of Queen's bridge.

Bonkers adjusted the hundred and fifty round carbon DSK on his lap and mugged the dark-skinned men that walked up and down the many blocks that they rolled past with their long dreads hanging and the masks of anger written across their faces. Some were even brazen enough to rock green and black Coronavirus masks, while others flat out wore the Jamaican flag as their face covering to protect them from the deadly Delta variant and to shield their identities. Bonkers shook his head in disgust and maintained his silence. The last thing he wanted to let Murda know was that he was both angry and a little worried about the play that Flocka was obviously displaying before them. When it came to the Game, the only time another man thought that it was cool for him to invade another man's territory and set up shop with his troops was when he no longer feared, respected, or carried about starting a war with him. Bonkers was under the impression that both he and Flocka had come to a great understanding amongst bosses, but to see that Flocka was setting his goons in place for a possible takeover was enough to send Bonkers into a slight frenzy.

Murda looked over at Bonkers as the rays of the sun shined brightly on to his forehead. He pulled down the visor and scanned the block they were rolling through. "So what's the call, kid? You thinking we should start spraying these fuck niggas every chance we get or what? Because I most definitely am. One thing I know about the homeboys from Jamrock is that once they get comfortable in a space, their next play is

45

take that bitch over. If we start exterminating they asses right now, I truly believe we can get a leg up on the war that's for sure brewing."

Bonkers nodded his head. "Yeah, that shit sound good if this was a ma'fuckin' movie or something like that but seeing as this is real life we can't move like that."

Reyanna grunted from the back seat. Everywhere she looked, she saw a Jamaican. This was odd to her. She got an eerie feeling deep within the pit of her gut. She clutched her .9 millimeter with the extended clip and grunted for a second time.

Bonkers looked into the back seat. "Shorty, what the fuck are you back there making all of that noise for?"

"For the first time about anythang, I agree with Murda." She curled her upper lip and continued to survey the situation outside of the Bentley truck as they rolled through block after block in Queens.

"You agree with him about what?" Bonkers side-eyed Murda, but kept his face toward Reyanna.

She continued, "It already look like that nigga Flocka is putting his men in place so that when he does come for Queens, there ain't gon' be much that we can really do about it other than fight to the death. I ain't never seen these many Jamaicans. They are literally on every fuckin' corner. How are they getting past immigration like this?"

Bonkers shrugged his shoulders. "I don't know, and I don't give a fuck. I'm about to set up a meeting with that fool Flocka right now to get to the bottom of this. Once I see where he's trying to go with things, then I'll make my decisions from there and not until then."

"Sounds to me like you're about to allow for another nigga to dictate how your operations are not only going to be run, but the longevity that's going to be attached to it. He can tell you anything. If you buy it, you ain't nothing but a straight sucka, word up." Reyanna was already growing irritated at his leadership skills. She knew that Kammron would have already started to murder the Jamaicans with no regard. Bonkers was starting to seem soft and way too timid for her. He needed more balls.

"Yo, hand to God, shorty, sometimes you be saying that shit that be making me want to slap the piss outta ya ass. Had you been any other bitch, I would have already. Ya tongue is serious!" Bonkers snapped. He turned back in his seat and started to survey Queens again, hating that Reyanna was more right than wrong.

"Nah, nigga, you just used to fake love. I ain't the type that's gone kiss ya ass and not tell you that you still got tissue all around ya crinkle back there. I'ma give it to you in the raw. I ain't feeling what I'm seeing. That nigga Killa would have already devised a plot to blow up the whole fuckin' Jamaica over seeing this shit. It's a double cross in the works and it looks like that shit is about to happen any day now. You lacking, B. Fuck what ya feelings is screaming at me right now, 'cause that shit ain't valid."

Bonkers turned back around to face her. "Bitch, did you really just bring that nigga Kammron up in my muthafuckin' whip? Huh? You comparing me to that nigga?"

Reyanna was silent for a moment. She thought about maintaining that silence, but then the Goddess within refused to cower. "Nigga, with everything you do, I scrutinize that ass because I done went from one regime to the next and I've seen what it looks like to be a part of a money-making, cutthroat, deadly crew of savages, and I gotta tell you quite honestly, what you got going on here ain't it."

Bonkers slapped her so fast that he didn't even know he was doing it until it was already done. The sounds echoed all around the truck. Reyanna ignored the pain and held her ground, eyeing him with hatred. Bonkers pointed his finger at her forehead. She didn't move. She knew he was feeling a way emotionally and she saw this as a major chink in his armor. The street veteran couldn't handle the truth without getting into his feelings, and that was a red flag for the level of the game that they were stepping into.

"Bitch, what the fuck are you still here for then, huh? Why don't you take yo' ratchet ass back over to the Coke Kings? I'm sure they'll welcome you with open arms right before they knock yo' fuckin' head off." He snickered and turned back around.

Reyanna sat there for a moment in silence. She could still feel the sting of the slap. She looked down at her gun and imagined taking the barrel and slamming it to the back of Bonkers head pulling the trigger. His brains would splatter all over the window. The earthy smell would fill the car along with gunpowder right before she'd hand Murda the same fate. She saw it all so clearly. An evil sneer came her face. But to act in such a way without grasping what she had up her sleeve would have been idiotic.

She sat back and maintained her composure just as Murda slammed on the brakes, causing her to hit he forehead on the back of Bonkers' seat. Four heavily-armed Jamaicans stepped in front of the truck. When the Bentley came to a full halt, four more came up behind it with rifles already drawn. Their faces were covered with their country's flag. Their dreads swung below their waist. They raised their weapons and aimed them at the trio inside of the truck.

Bonkers cursed under his breath. "What the fuck is this shit about?"

A dark-skinned Jamaican with light gray eyes stepped up to Murda's window and knocked on the glass. He signed for

Murda to roll down the window. When Murda complied, he stuck his ugly face into the truck, reeking of sandalwood. "Dis iz far as you go wit' no clearance from above. Turn around or we have to gun ya down right now."

Bonkers looked into the man's face and glared at him. "Say, Blood, who the fuck you work under?"

The Jamaican waved him off. "Dis iz dee last warning. No clearance, no pass. Turn around."

"Say, nigga, if you working for Flocka you betta get that ugly gorilla on the phone and tell him that Bonkers said you out here fuckin' up and about to cause a deadly war, my dude. Yo' best bet is to get the fuck out of the way before all of this shit turn real tragic."

The Jamaican lowered his eyes. A broad smile crossed his lips. "So ya know Flocka, yeah?"

"You muthafuckin' right!" Bonkers retorted. "Now get the fuck out of the way before that fool order me to drill yo' ass."

The Jamaican laughed. "Awright, well, me didn't know dat you knew dee king. Gon' right ahead down dat way dare." He pointed and stepped to the side lowering his weapon.

"Now dat's more like it." Bonkers settled in his seat and waved Murda to drive on.

Murda hesitated. "Yo, I ain't feeling dis, kid. I think we should just turn around. Ain't shit else to see in Queens anyway. We already know what it is."

"Who the fuck is the boss nigga? Huh? It's me, right?" Bonkers hollered, feeling his blood pressure go through the roof.

"Without a doubt," Murda assured him.

"Then go forward. Don't do shit else but that," Bonkers ordered.

"Awright, Dunn." Murda eased off of the brake and the truck began to move.

Reyanna kept her eyes on the commanding Jamaican at all times. Something wasn't right about him. When she saw him give the signal for his troops to start shooting before he himself cocked and aimed his weapon, she went into action. Before he could get a good shot off on Bonkers, she was bussing through the back window, sending three deadly slugs that smacked into the side of the Jamaican's head and twisted him around before he fell to his knees in a pool of blood and brain matter. She sank to the floor of the truck once the shooters that had them surrounded began to dump their bullets into the truck. Murda stormed off and flew through the stop sign. He didn't get more than twenty feet before he slammed into an ice cream truck coming from the east. The Bentley's metal made a nasty sound before it came to a stop and began to smoke. The bullets from the enemy kept coming. Murda hollered that he was hit more than once.

His foot slammed on the gas, causing the car to jerk violently before it hopped the curb and clipped a fire hydrant. Bonkers' head slammed forward and smashed into the dashboard. The airbag deployed, though he was already knocked out cold.

"I can feel blood oozing down my back! Fuck, this shit hurt!" He swerved a few times before they jolted out onto the busy intersection. Cars blew their horns and navigated to miss their vehicle. More shots came their way. Reyanna's window exploded. Glass landed all inside of her lap and over her face. Murda drove the truck onto the grassy boulevard and fainted from the blood loss. Two Jamaicans jumped out of the car from across the street with guns in their hands, looking to finish the trio off.

Chapter 7

Reyanna saw the two men right away. Her heart began to beat faster and faster. She smacked the back of Murda's seat. "Yo, Murda, wake ya ass up and pull off! Those niggas coming to drill our ass." She smacked the seat again and then the back of his head. "Yo, Murda, I ain't playing, get ya ass up!"

Murda was in a faraway zone. Bonkers came to. Blood poured out of his nose onto his chest. He grabbed his head with both hands and looked down at the airbag with confusion. He frowned his face and closed his eyes again.

Reyanna hurried to the front of the truck just as a slug crashed into and shattered Bonkers' window. "Shit, these muthafuckas coming! Murda, you gotta get the fuck out of the way!" She pulled him from his seat and tossed him to the floor just under the console. Murda groaned and curled into a ball. Reyanna opened the driver's door and stepped out. She began to aim and fire at the men from over the top of the truck with round after round.

Boom. Boom. Boom. Boom.

The Jamaicans ducked for cover. They stopped to fire back at her, walking backward into the street. Pedestrians screamed and ran to get out of the way of the gunfire as more bullets zipped back and forth seemingly aimlessly.

Reyanna bucked her gun until it shook empty with smoke coming from it. She jumped inside of the truck and threw it into drive, stepping on the gas immediately. The tires kicked up smoke and turf before it wiggled back on to the street. Once there, Reyanna sped away with slugs slamming into the body of the truck again and again. "Those punk-ass Jamaicans! That's who the fuck we're supposed to be linked up with? Huh, those guys? That makes no sense."

Bonkers cringed and held his bleeding shoulder. "Bitch-ass niggas! I'ma get to the bottom of this shit real good, you better believe that. I ain't taking this shit lying down. That bitch nigga Flocka got some explaining to do. You can bet that."

Reyanna side-eyed him. She looked down at Murda and saw that he was unmoving, yet there was a puddle of blood under him. "I think Murda dead as hell. There is so much blood over here that it's seeping into my socks."

Bonkers unhooked his seat belt and got to the Bentley's floor beside Murda. He pulled him out of the ball and placed his finger on to his neck. He lowered his head. "Damn, the homie was young as a bitch." He closed Murda's eyes and rolled him into the back of the truck. "Yo, pull over, shorty by that alley up there."

"By the alley? For what?"

"This nigga dead. We gotta get him the fuck out of here, we're already driving around with bullet holes all in the body of the truck. I'm surprised we ain't got pulled over yet."

"So you just gon' dump ya mans out on the street? Ain't that nigga at least worth a proper burial?"

"Nah, bruh ain't got no family like that. All the ma'fuckas that would probably attend his funeral been ducking the Feds for a minute now, or the state trying to jam them up on murders all across the spectrum. Ain't no funerals happening in Queens unless it's for a crazy circumstance like a shorty getting hit up a somethin'. So pull over the fuckin' whip."

Reyanna pulled the truck into the alley and stopped half-way inside of it. "Hurry up. I get an eerie feeling being in this janky-ass alley."

"Shut up! Fuck you think, I'ma slow walk the mission a somethin'?"

Reyanna rolled her eyes. "Just hurry up, boy."

Bonkers opened the side door and jumped out into the warm atmosphere. The sky was slowly darkening. Down the way, the sounds of two alley cats fighting each other with extreme hatred was loud and boisterous. The scent was spoiled garbage and gasoline. Bonkers grabbed Murda's legs and pulled him out of the truck recklessly. Murda fell out of it with the back of his head cracking open against the concrete. Bonkers cursed under his breath and kept pulling Murda until he had him ducked off in an open, empty garage. He laid him out the long way and hustled back to the truck. As he was coming out of the garage, a squad car was turning into the alley slowly after witnessing the Bentley turn into the drug-infested alleyway. Unbeknownst to Reyanna and Bonkers this same squadron had only ten minutes ago chased away a slew of drug dealers. Bonkers paused when he saw the police car with his eyes as big as saucers.

"Nigga, get ya ass in. What the fuck is you freezing and looking all crazy for? We gotta go - now!"

Bonkers shook his head as hard as he could before climbing back inside of the truck. He absentmindedly forgot to close the backdoors. Reyanna pulled off. The police car came all the way into the alley and stopped right in front of the open garage. The police officer beamed his big light that was located on the side of his squad car into the interiors of Murda's dump place. When the spotlight scanned them over the sirens were flipped on.

"Got damn it!" Reyanna stepped on the gas and made a sharp left as soon as she exited the alley. She accelerated the Bentley as fast as it could go, leaving the squad car a block behind. She made a right at the next corner, and then a left at the one that followed that one before she turned into an alley and flew down it. As soon as she found another open garage, she turned into it and cut the ignition. "We gotta get the hell out of here right now, Bonkers. Come on." She said this while exiting the vehicle.

Bonkers was right behind her. They ran out of the garage and jumped two fences back to back, ignoring the Dobermans that were in the yard of one of them. Before the dogs could even think to get close, they were already running down a side street and watching one police car after the next zoom down the block north of the one they were on. It didn't take long for Bonkers to get out of breath, especially because he had been grazed in the shootout and was losing a significant amount of blood. "Yo, Reyanna, damn, girl, I can't fucking breathe, slow up." He hunched over with his hands on his knees.

Reyanna slowed just enough to not disappear from him. She was in flight for life mode. There was no way that she was about to do life in prison for something that she didn't do. Her eyes scanned the dark neighborhood, looking for an escape route. "Yo, this is bananas, B. I don't even know where the fuck we are."

"We're in Queen's Bridge. The Kings run this section and they don't fuck wit' our kind, so we better get the fuck up out of here quick," Bonkers warned.

"That's a given." She stepped out into the street just as twenty Latinos seemed to come out of every gangway. Each of them had gold bandanas across their faces and a Glizzy in their hands. Reyanna lowered her head and stayed in place. She wondered how the day could get any worse.

Bonkers wiped sweat from his forehead. He had an F&N on him, but knew that it was pointless to raise it. They were outnumbered and outgunned. He raised his hands. "Bruh, look, we didn't come here on no fuck shit. We on the run from the Jake and this was our only escape route. Please let us pass. Y'all do, and I'll come back and drop fifty K, that's word to my borough."

A heavyset man with a five point star on the left side of his face stepped up Bonkers and looked him up and down. "The shit we'll do to you over here for stepping on sacred ground is far worse than what a pig could ever do. Then you hollering about fifty G's? Bitch, that's walking around money." He pulled out a sixty thousand dollar knot and placed it to Bonkers' nose. "You smell that shit?"

Bonkers remained still. "Yeah, nigga, I do."

The Spanish man put the money back in his pocket and placed the barrel of his gun to Bonkers' cheek. "You cuz, nigga? Or wait a minute, let me guess, you gotta be a Choo nigga? N'all, maybe you one of those whack-ass Woo niggas. Where the fuck you from kid?"

"Harlem, by way of Queens," Bonkers answered with the click of Latin Kings surrounding him and Reyanna with deathly intent.

"Bitch, red or blue? Fuck you banging?" the obvious leader asked.

"Green, nigga. I don't bang for no color other than green, and if fifty bands ain't enough, then tell me your price. Say dat shit and I'll pay dat shit, word up." Bonkers was willing to negotiate any price as long as he was able to leave the bidding with his life and Reyanna's life intact.

"Red or blue, nigga. You gotta be one?" the leader reiterated.

"Yo, we ain't banging neither one of those dumb sets. We from Queens, nigga. We get money. We stay in our own lane. How many times my mans here I gotta tell you that shit?" Reyanna said this in Spanish for all to comprehend.

The leader gasped and turned his attention to her. He walked into her face just as it began to drizzle outside. "Aw, we got us a li'l tough mamacita right here, don't we?" He ran his eyes all over her body and licked his lips. "And what a mamacita do we have?"

"Yo, let us go, Dunn. We got places to be and shit. You niggas know we don't want it wit' y'all. Y'all ain't our enemies. We got love for the Kings, word to Queens. We just got caught up in a sticky. That shit happens. We got fifty for the inconvenience. That's it; that's all."

"Yo, Reyanna, chill wit' ya tongue, shorty, and humble ya'self," Bonkers ordered.

"N'all, fuck that. You see, I like a fine bitch with some balls like this one got right here." He looked over again and nodded his head. "Yeah, baby, what else you got on your chest that you wanna get off?"

"Nothing. Y'all need to let us go though. We gotta get the fuck out of this area." She said this looking around nervously. She could hear sirens off in the distance.

The leader stepped closer to her again. He ran his hands all over her frame while she closed her eyes and cringed at his touch. "You got that Latin shit in you, don't you, ma? I mean, you got way too much heart to not have it in you." He gripped her ass.

Reyanna pushed him as hard as she could. "Get the fuck off of me, Dunn! I don't know you like that."

The leader busted up laughing. "Yo, this broad is comical as fuck. Check it: get this black nigga the fuck off of our turf and snatch this li'l pretty bitch up. I think she'll look better as a Queen, and I gotta have her. Ain't no way around that."

Bonkers backed up as a group of men surrounded him with their guns aimed at his head. He held up his hands in surrender. "Yeah, a'ight, let me go then."

Reyanna was grabbed from behind and a massive arm was wrapped around her neck. She fought against it. "Let me go!" she hollered as soon as she got room to utter a word.

"N'all, bitch, you're trapped in the barrio now. Say good bye to this nigga. Last time you see him is the last time he'll see you."

T.J. Edwards

Chapter 8

"I don't give a fuck how many times the don done felt this type of treatment. The shit never gets old." Kammron said this as he laid back while two shapely half naked Brazilian women gave his body a once over, grooming him from head to toe. Kammron gripped both of their asses and slipped his finger in between their G strings with a smile on his face.

Henny laid on her stomach and enjoyed her massage that the small Brazilian teen gave to her. It took all of the discipline that she had in herself to ignore Kammron and the women that he had tending to him. She slightly shook her head. Kammron could never keep things professional. It there was a woman involved, he always had to make things sexual. That entire facet of things was getting on her nerves. "Yeah, Killa, well how about you keep it quiet over there. I'm trying to enjoy my massage right now."

Kammron sat up and drank half of the Ducè that he'd been nursing for over an hour. He felt the Percocets starting to over-power his system, and that brought a sudden surge of adrenalin to him. He hopped off of the table and allowed for his towel to fall to the ground, exposing his nakedness. "Yo, fuck this. Close that door over there, mami. I'm about to tax every ass in this bitch. Word is bond. You South Americans running around looking too good for the kid to pass up, so I gotta have that ass."

The darker-skinned Brazilian stepped over and locked the door. She placed her back to it with her eyes never leaving the sight of his long penis that swung from left to right as he took a few steps to give out his orders.

"You gon' get us in trouble, Mr. Giles. What if we get caught?" she asked in her broken English.

Kammron grabbed a bundle of cash out of his Gucci knapsack. "Yo, fuck what ya worried about. I got fifty gees right here to fuck off. Now you bitches really worried about what the hell ya boss gon' be screaming knowing you'll probably never see this kind of cash ever in your life, or you trying to get this cream?" He looked them over, stroking his piece, which began to swell.

The one that locked the door appeared frozen. She looked over to her partner. "What we gon' do?"

The Brazilian that was massaging Kammron's shoulders walked over and dropped down to her knees in front of him. She looked up at him with her green eyes shimmering. She took ahold of his dick and stroked it. "Whatever you want, I'm game." She licked her lips and prepared to receive him.

Kammron grabbed a handful of her hair and looked down at her with amusement. He nodded and drank from his bottle before slipping into her mouth. The heat caused him to groan loudly. He shivered and closed his eyes for a moment. Her face moved faster and faster in his lap, making loud slurping noises. When Kammron opened his eyes again, Henny was up and mugging him with anger. Kammron blew a kiss at her.

"Yo, word is bond, this li'l bitch got the craziest head I done ever had. She can't be no older than eighteen too. Ain't that a bitch?"

Henny mugged her, and then shot daggers at the girl's co-worker as the girl dropped to her knees beside her. In a matter of seconds, they were both fighting over who was going to put Kammron's dick into their mouth. First one would suck him, and then the other would grab it out of the other's hand and she'd fellate him loudly and as whorishly as she could to one-up her friend.

Kammron sat on the couch and allowed for the women to continue to please him. He poured the liquor all over their heads. Their hair curled up even more. They growled and moaned as they sucked him. The younger of the two stood up and ran her fingers through her coochie lips. Her golden folds separated before her middle finger slipped inside of her. The sight of Kammron's big dick was enough to create a hunger within her middle. "I want him to fuck me right now."

Kammron cheesed. "Yo, you feening for the pipe, huh, ma?"

She nodded and rubbed her pussy juices all over her nipples, pulling them. She sucked her bottom lip. "I want him now."

Her friend stroked his dick faster and faster before she sucked it into her mouth. She took ahold of it with her breasts and masturbated him that way for a full minute. When she eased backward, his dick was throbbing as if it was seconds away from exploding.

The younger of the two came over and straddled his waist with her juicy booty in the air, and her long curls flowing down her back. Kammron pulled her cheeks apart to expose the two holes that her globes shielded. Her pussy was oozing its secretions all over his lap. She rose and reached under herself to take ahold of his penis. Once she had it in her hands, she squeezed it and ran the head around her opening. When she slid down and sat on his balls, Kammron groaned in her ear and then bit her on the neck, causing her to scream and cum that easily. Kammron allowed for her tremors to subside before he began to move her up and down his dick again and again.

The girl's friend stuck her face between their sexing parts, licking all over them. She slurped and would suck Kammron's dick into her mouth every time it fell out of her friend, all slimy and full of pussy juices. She had two fingers up her own pussy, working herself over in a fashion that had white foam leaking out of her.

"Uhhhhh! Uhhhhh! Un-huh! Un-huh! Shit, baby!" the younger of the two screamed.

Kammron clenched his teeth as the feeling of the girl's pussy seemed to get better and better. He slammed her down twenty hard times in a row before he bussed off in her, growling like a vicious lion on the kill. "Fuck, fuck, fuck, bitch!" He pushed her off of him and stood up, jerking his piece shooting semen all over her, before her friend sucked him into her mouth.

Henny got up from the massage table and grabbed the first girl by her hair. She slammed her against the wall. "Bitch, you better not have no fuckin' diseases, because if you gave my nigga anything, I swear to God I'ma kill yo' ass. You, that bitch that he finna fuck over there, and anybody else that get in my way. I ain't playing neither. So tell me now, do you got anything?"

She shook her head. "No! Now get off of me." She pushed Henny out of her face, sending her stumbling backwards.

The female that had been massaging Henny hopped up and stood protectively between Henny and the younger worker. She mugged Henny. "You have to leave. Now!"

Henny balled both of her fists. "You ain't got no right putting her hands on me."

"You touch me first 'cause you jealous," the younger girl stated.

Henny pointed at her. "Bitch, I ain't jealous of shit."

Kammron had the other girl bent over the massage table, fucking her like an animal. He grabbed ahold of her hips and pounded into her again and again, faster and faster. His dick was like a battering ram while he grunted, fingering the woman's booty at the same time.

Henny noticed the sounds and looked over at the sexing pair. This infuriated her even more. She wondered if Kammron had any respect for her at all, because it surely seemed as if he did not. "Kammron, let's go!"

Kammron ignored her. He pulled out and turned the thick woman around, slamming her on the table and forcing her knees to her chest while he fucked her with long strokes, digging deeper and deeper. She sat up and licked all over his neck. Her teeth nipped at his tender skin. She bit him and sucked as hard as she could. Kammron shivered and really began to fuck her harder and harder.

The two females blocked Henny's path as she began to make her way over to Kammron. The older of the two spoke up. "Hey, you have to leave the building right now. You had no right creating the conflict that you did."

Henny waved her off. "Bitch, move. I ain't tryna hear that shit. I'm 'bout to get my nigga and we're both about to get the fuck up out of here." She saw Kammron and the woman kissing and this for some unexplained reason made her feel as if she was about to throw up. Kammron rarely ever kissed her. "Kammron, we gotta go."

Kammron plunged seven hard times and groaned at the top of his lungs, then he felt his seed shooting out of him in thick spurts. He opened his mouth wide and fell chest to chest with the woman, jerking like crazy.

Henny hurried over and pulled him off of her. "Nigga, I said bring ya ass on."

Kammron snatched away from her. He stood up and poured the rest of the alcohol all over her head. "Bitch, yo' li'l ass always so hot and heated. Calm yo' muthafuckin' ass down."

Henny stood there feeling like a fool. She could hear the women laughing all around her, and this only heightened her anger toward the injustice that Kammron had forced upon her. She wiped her face clean of the alcohol and looked up at him. "Really, Killa? This is how you're going to do me in front of these bitches?"

Kammron was high as a kite. He staggered a bit and tapped the bottle of the bottle so that another drip came out and splashed onto her forehead, then he took his tongue and licked all around the opening of the bottle. "Everywhere we go that got a few hoes, you never know how to act. I'm tired of that shit. Get yo'self together before I drop you. Word is bond."

Now the other females were really laughing and whispering amongst themselves in Portuguese. Henny mugged all three of them and felt humiliated. She was about to cut her losses when she noticed a thick line of semen drip down the female's thigh that Kammron had fucked last. The woman caught it and rubbed the remnants into her pussy's opening before sucking her fingers. Henny snapped.

She screamed and rushed across the room, taking ahold of the woman's hair and slamming her to the ground with all of her might. Once there, she stomped her in the face four quick times.

"Aw, hell n'all!" the youngest of the three hollered. She made a beeline for Henny.

Henny met her head on. Before the girl could do anything, Henny was punching her so hard in the chin that she knocked her out cold. The girl wound up laying on her side, snoring loudly.

"She's crazy!" the third chick yelled, running out of the room.

Henny stepped into Kammron's face. "Nigga, let's go! I ain't gon' say dis shit no more."

Kammron looked her up and down and sucked his teeth re slowly, but loud enough for the effects of his antics to set in.

"Yo, word is bond, bitch, I'ma let you have this one. I will say that you starting to get way too big for ya britches though. Let me grab my shit and we gon' get up out of here."

Henny watched him in action, slightly nodding her head. *I'm so tired of this fool tryna size me up just to make a clown of me. I don't know what he thank this is, but I gotta trick for all of this, baby daddy or not*, she thought as she waited for Kammron to grab all of his things before they left and drove back to Harlem in silence.

T.J. Edwards

Chapter 9

"Yo, I still ain't understanding the reason y'all got us down here for, Dunn. If it's about the money, y'all niggas still ain't put a price on shit. I ain't understanding the science behind this money ball, word up," Bonkers snapped while looking over the handcuffs that were attached to his wrist.

There was a short chain that bound him and Reyanna to the brick wall of the basement. There were large rats screeching as they trampled underfoot. Cockroaches assailed the bricks. Big spiderwebs that were inhabited by humongous spiders posted up in the corners. The basement smelled like sour milk. There was dried blood all over the concrete along with a few rotten teeth from the last opposition the Kings had brought down into the basement. The opp had never been seen or heard from again.

Peachy, a 6'5" Mexican, came down the stairs fitted in black and gold Gucci. He puffed on a stuffed Dutch Master and held an all-black Draco in his right hand. He stepped into Bonkers' face and blew a cloud of smoke into it. "Word is that you been running these soup coolers for the last four hours, wondering why the fuck you are in the Opps Final Destination. Dat true?"

Bunkers raised his right eye brow. "What the fuck are you talking about? I don't even know where the fuck that is."

Peachy laughed. "You're chained inside of it, homes, and one thang I can say about when a ma'fucka show up here is that it's their final destination. Shit ain't looking too good for you, especially if yo' stamp don't come back from a few of my compadres in Queens. You betta hope that any real nigga that's slimed in wit' us know who the fuck Bonkers is, and next to that, you betta hope that they ain't viewing you as the

Opp, 'cause we'll sell yo body quicker than a ma'fucka caught up in a sex trafficking ring, straight like that."

"I don't give a fuck who you slimed in wit'. If they from Queens, then they know what it is wit' me. I am Queens," Bonkers boasted.

"Nigga, we're about to see real quick here. Besides all of that, what the fuck are y'all doing in Crown Town?"

"We got jammed up by a couple opps that caught my mans lacking. A li'l crash took place while we were trying to slide up out of here, and in the process, we wound up having to truck it on foot. Yo' people surrounded us during this endeavor, and the rest is common sense," Bonkers told him while adjusting the cuffs that were on his wrist.

Peachy rubbed his chin as he listened. "Awright, I get all of that. Now explain to me what gives you the fuckin' right to be dropping off dead bodies in my barrio? Don't you know that every time a body drops over here, the Feds try to find a way to pin that shit on my crew?"

"How the fuck are we supposed to know any of that shit right there, huh? We just met you niggas earlier today? We ain't got shit to do wit' no Kings, none of y'all opps, and yet y'all still got us down here and shit. What the fuck is the problem? 'Cause I'm not understanding?" Reyanna snapped, irritated after killing the second cockroach that had crawled up her leg. She wanted out and didn't comprehend what the Kings had up their sleeves if it wasn't about the money.

Peachy got so close to her that they were lip to lip. He smiled and took a hit of his blunt before turning his back on her. "Yo, she remind me of one of the Queens out here. You sure you ain't rocking a crown on ya head, ma?"

"N'all, I'm repping Queens by way of Harlem all day every day. I don't got nothing against yo' gang and all of that shit right there, but loyalties lie where they do. Why you ain't tryna let my mans drop a bundle in ya lap so we can navigate up out of this situation? We ain't got shit against y'all."

"Yo, this mama seem like she got more heart, and more common sense, than you do, Bonkers. You sho' she ain't the one that's running Queens over there, huh? Maybe I should ask the streets who she is instead of you. Maybe I'll get more responses than what I'm getting for you right now."

Reyanna didn't want him to do that because she knew that there was a million dollar price tag on her head for trying to kill Kammron. As far as she knew she had killed him because nobody had gotten back to her and told her whether Kammron was deceased or not, but at the same time, she cursed herself for not making any lasting connections while she rotated over in Harlem because after he transgression against him she had been cut out of the loop immediately and that hurt worse than a series of paper cuts.

"Yo, quit all of that disrespectful shit, B. I ain't capped at yo' deck one time. I'm from Queens, nigga, but more than anything, I'm a Harlem nigga first and for most. We don't let bitches run shit. Let's get that clear, word up." Bonkers felt himself heating up.

Peachy rubbed the side of Reyanna's face until she cringed and pulled her head away. "To be honest, I don't give a fuck what the opps do on they decks. Over here had we a Queen like this, I'd make sure that she bagged twenty-five thousand a week, and that everything was paid for as long as it had something to do with her. Not only would she be in a position of power, but I would have her making major moves. You see, over this way we don't stress about that gender shit. It's all about leadership, and this mami right here got all of that, word is bond. I can see that, yo."

Bonkers shrugged his shoulders. "Nigga, den let me go and you can keep the bitch."

Reyanna lowered her eyes. "Excuse you?"

Peachy laughed. "You sho 'bout that?" He rested his Draco up against his shoulder. "If I had her on my team, I can't see myself being fucked with. On some real shit, that's all I'm missing."

"Take her then. I'm serious as a heart attack. I got shit that I gotta attend to." Bonkers refused to make eye contact with Reyanna. He was in a state of desperation and he needed to do whatever he had to in order to come from out the trenches. He didn't truly meant what he said about Reyanna, but he could see by the way that Peachy was looking at her that he obviously had a crazy liking to her, and it was in Bonkers' best interest to use that to the best of his ability - at least, that was how he felt.

"So you mean to tell me that she ain't worth shit to you homie? Not nothing?" Peachy asked.

"Not more than myself. It's a million bitches at the god's feet. Fuck I look like chasing one?" Bonkers spat.

"Wow." Reyanna lowered her head. She had never felt more insulted.

Peachy held up one finger as his phone rang. He placed it to his ear. "Yeah, this nigga got waves, dark brown complexion, and all of that. Matter fact..." He held up his phone and took a picture of Bonkers. "Yo, you got it?" He waited for a response. When he got it, he laughed with his head tilted backward. "That figures. Yo, you owe me one, slime, word up. Gang gang." He looked over to his crew of demons. "Let that nigga loose. Ole girl too. I just got word that he stamped. We can't bury they ass this time, but next time y'all get caught lacking in Crown Town, I'ma be forced to have my niggas slide on you, word up."

Bonkers waited until the cuffs were off of his wrists before he rubbed the spots were they had at once been. He mugged

Peachy. "Whose yo' source, Dunn? Who the fuck you call to check up on me. I am Queens."

Peachy laughed. "Seems to me that you ain't nothing but a pawn my nigga." He stepped over to Reyanna and personally took her cuffs off one at a time. "Yo, you sure that you don't wanna get stamped over here wit' me, mami? I promise you royalty."

Reyanna placed a thick tuft of curly hair behind her ear and smiled weakly at him. "I guess I'm too loyal to a fault, but thank you for the offer though. I can tell that you would honestly know how to treat a woman like me."

Bonkers sucked his teeth. "Yo, let's get the fuck up out of here before you two get married. This movie starting to make me feel sick to the stomach, word up."

***

When they got into the third story walk-up inside of Queens, Reyanna waited until Bonkers stepped inside of it before she came down and slammed the door so hard that the wood around the door jamb splintered. "I can't believe you!"

Bonkers jumped and turned around with a vicious mug on his face. "Man! What the fuck is wrong with you?"

Reyanna was so angry that before she could control and stop them from coming the tears were already pouring down her cheeks. "You said all of that stuff back there. You made me feel like I ain't worth shit to you. You was ready to let them keep me and you was acting like you didn't give a rat's ass what they did with me! What is yo' problem?!"

Bonkers pulled his nose and mugged her with his anger mounting. He made his way in her direction with his finger pointed at her face. "Look, I don't know what the fuck yo' problem is, but I'ma tell you just like this. When it comes down to survival, a ma'fucka gotta say whatever he needs to in order to pull himself up out of that jam. Half the shit I said I didn't mean. That was cap."

Reyanna shook her head slowly. "It sho didn't feel like cap. It felt like everything that you said you actually meant. I didn't see a shred of compassion or concern for myself in your eyes when you were speaking. All I saw was selfishness, and self-absorption. Those actions were so reminiscent."

Bonkers poked her chest with his finger. "There you go with that comparing me to Kammron shit. How many times gotta tell yo' ass that that's somethin' that we just ain't gon' do?"

Reyanna turned her back to him. "I don't know what I was even thinking. Why did I come here? How could I expect for you to be any different than him when you two were raised side by side together?"

"See! You still doing that shit!" He turned her around so that she was facing him again. "Yo, I told you about comparing me to the same nigga that fucked me over in so any ways that I don't even wanna begin to talk about that shit, yet you are still doing it. When will you get it through your head that every time you put me and him in the same category that you bring that demon shit out of me?"

Reyanna backed up and shook her head. She pointed her finger in his face now. "Nigga, I don't care about none of that. I call it how I sees it, and what I see is the same mean, disrespectful, self-centered, egotistical jerk that Kammron was. You don't treat me no better than he did, and like for him, I ain't shown you nothing but loyalty. I ain't about to get fucked over twice. I'm done playing that game." She turned her back on him again and started to gather her things from around the apartment while Bonkers mugged her, clenching his fists.

Chapter 10

"So what, you call yo'self about to leave a nigga a somethin'?" Bonkers asked as he watched her go all around the living room stuffing miscellaneous items of hers into a big Dooney and Burke suitcase.

"Bonkers, at this point, I don't know what to say to you. If all of that bullshit that you exposed to those Latin dudes don't mean nothing to you, then it don't mean nothing to me either, but I'd be a damn fool to stay here knowing how you really feel about me. I need to take some time out to get my bearings. I can't cope right now."

Bonkers stood there for a moment just watching her pack more and more things into the suitcase. He imagined what it would have looked like for her to stand over Kammron and to deliver a series of deadly slugs into his body before she made her grand escape. He imagined Kammron's blood filling the bathroom as she said it had, and that brought an evil smile to his face. There was no way that he could let her go. In fact, the sight of her was one of the strongest reasons he kept her around. Her presence was like a walking Kammron tombstone.

She walked past Bonkers, headed into the backroom of the house. "Excuse me." When she got there, she took a deep breath to settle herself, then she was stuffing more of her things inside of the suitcase.

Bonkers came to the door frame and stood there seething. "Yo, for a bitch that done put a nigga in the dirt not too long ago, you sho' acting all emotional and shit. Why the fuck you all up in yo' feels?"

Reyanna grunted. "It's just sad that you don't know why, Bonkers. That just goes to show that you aren't as observant as you think you are."

"What, bitch? That ain't an answer. Speak English."

Reyanna rolled her eyes. She stuffed the suitcase as much as she could, grabbed twenty thousand dollars from out of her pillowcase located on her side of the bed, and got ready to leave.

Bonkers slipped in front of her and refused to make eye contact with her. "Shorty, I ain't about to let you go nowhere, word is bond. Fuck that."

Reyanna furrowed her eyebrows. "Yo, Bonkers, get ya black ass out the way. Come on now, I ain't playin' wit' you." She started to walk through the doorway again.

Bonkers tensed his muscles. "Take that shit that you got in that suitcase and find somewhere to sit yo' half-breed ass down. You ain't about to go nowhere. That's final, and don't make me say that shit again."

Reyanna looked up and into his brown eyes that were avoiding her, looking every which way. "Yo, kid, move ya ass. I ain't about to do this with you right now. I need to blow this joint so I can go and get some understanding alone. I need to take a few weeks and just chill and all of that. I ain't feeling this set-up right now."

"I don't care about none of that shit you kicking. You ain't going nowhere. You already know what you signed up for. This is what it is." He tried to grab the suitcase out of her hand.

Reyanna pulled it back. "Nigga, watch out." She gasped in distaste. "How dare you? Now you wanna act like you feeling a way 'cause I'm about to leave when just hours ago you was ready to leave me to fend for myself around a bunch of low lives that probably don't have shit on their minds other than raping me. God, Bonkers, what type of man is you anyway?"

"Man, them pussies wasn't about to do none of that."

"Oh yeah? And how the fuck do you know? 'Cause you sho' was ready to roll the dice to find out."

"Because I know. I been in the field ever since I was eleven years old. I know stone cold killers and rapists when I see 'em and I'm telling you that Peachy wasn't on that shit wit' you. If I'ma keep shit a whole buck, that fool really liked ya ass, and I could see him trying to wife you 'cause he don't know the real you, you know. All that shit that I really do know and I'm still fucking wit' you the long way."

Reyanna sighed and placed her hand on her hip. "What about all of the shit that I know about you? Huh? Yo' history most definitely ain't no mystery."

"I don't care about what you know. I'm god body, shorty. Like I said before, I been in the field since a young'un. It is what it is. The bottom line is that you ain't about to go nowhere. That's what that is right there. Now give me the suitcase."

"Ain't." She pulled it back and took a step in the same direction.

Bonkers started to get heated. "Yo, stop playin' wit' me 'fore I beat yo' ass. Give me that shit and that money you took out of my pillowcase." He reached for the suitcase again.

Reyanna took three steps back. "Now yo' ass is really tripping. Nigga I ain't about to give you one red cent. That money is mine. I brought it with me, and you ain't about to stop me from going nowhere. I ain't yo' woman."

"Ugh! Never that. The most you could ever be is my bitch. I ain't making no broad my woman that Kammron done touched - not now not ever!"

Reyanna stomped her right foot. "That's it!" She tightened her hand on the suitcase and made a beeline straight for the exit of the bedroom. "Get the fuck out of my way! I'm done wit' you, Bonkers, wit' yo' rude ass."

Bonkers waited until she crashed into him before he slipped beside her and tripped her by sticking his leg behind hers. He pushed her hard. She came crashing to the floor with so much impact that it knocked the wind out of her. "I told you to stop playin' wit' me. Yo' ass is hard-headed." He opened the suitcase and flung the clothes and all of the rest of her things all around the room. "The next time you even thank about leaving me' I'ma drill yo ass."

Reyanna coughed harshly and crawled to her knees. She used the wall to get to her feet and once there, she balled her fists and lowered her eyes. "So think it's that sweet huh?" she asked with her voice raspy and her eyes watering. "You think that you're about to leave me trapped in this house like some punk bitch?"

Bonkers nodded. "Bitch, yeah, I do. Clean up this shit, and get yo' ass in there and whip up some of that Spanish shit that you be whipping. Hurry up."

Reyanna shook her head with tears rolling down her cheeks. "I ain't about to let you treat me like that. I'd rather die first. If you want me to do what you're saying, you gon' have to whoop my ass, 'cause I ain't going. Never that." She raised her guards higher. "Let's go, Bonkers, me and you nigga, me and YOU!"

She rushed him at full speed, swinging with precision. While Bonkers slapped away her left hook, he got caught with her right jab. The pain shocked him. She followed with another left hook that connected with his jaw and a right straight that knocked him over the couch. He felt like stars were circling around the top of his head.

"Get up! Get up, Bonkers, I'm ready!"

Bonkers came to his knees seeing double. He shook his head as hard as he could. When he came to his feet, he staggered a bit. "I'm finna fuck you up, bitch. See, you thank 'cause you put that nigga down that it gives you the right to step all the way in the field, but I'm about to show yo' ass. You can't fuck wit' a real ma'fuckas bidness." He was lucid again. He scanned the room for her and found her. His double vision had disappeared. He hopped over the couch and threw up his guards, closing in on her with them raised protectively of his mug the closer he got to her.

Reyanna didn't wait. She closed the gap and started swinging like her life depended on it. Most of her attacks were blocked. She kept going at him. When she felt herself being raised into the air she yelped. The next she knew she was being thrown across the room and into the wall. She groaned in pain and forced herself to get back up.

Bonkers caught her just about standing. He grabbed a handful of her hair and slapped her with so much steam that she dropped to her knees. In doing so, Reyanna head-butted him in the nuts, dropping him right beside her. Both squirmed around on the carpet trying to figure out their next move. Reyanna used the couch to begin to assist her to her feet. Bonkers grabbed her hair again and flung her to the ground. She screamed from the pain. Bonkers rolled on top of her and held her wrists to the carpet while she kicked and twisted wildly.

"You too wild for yo' own good. Word is bond, if I didn't have a liking for you, I would have put a slug right through yo fuckin' face. Don't you get that?"

Reyanna tossed and turned from right to left. "Let me up! Get the fuck off of me!"

"You must thank it's a game, huh?" Bonkers became irate. He released one of her wrists long enough to slap her across the face.

Blood oozed out of Reyanna's nose. She closed her eyes and stayed still for a moment. "Bonkers, please let me up. I don't wanna do this with you no more. I'm done fighting. You want me to go and cook ya ass some chorizo, I will. Just please release me."

Bonkers held her a tad bit longer to make sure that there was no more resistance coming from her. Then he jumped up and dusted off his Prada fit. His nose was also bleeding. "I ain't gon' lie, yo' li'l ass got heart."

Reyanna rose and straightened out her Fendi skirt dress. "What would you like to eat?"

"Yo, I'm sorry about that shit I said. I ain't mean none of it, word to the borough, I didn't."

Reyanna wiped her nose with the back of her hand and saw that it was full of blood. "I'ma go shower, then I'ma cook breakfast. That's what that's going to be, Bonkers."

She walked away from him in silence, a million devious things running through her mind.

Chapter 11

"Yo god, you should have seen that nigga face. He was so worried about one of the gang slumping him that he offered up the mixed bitch as a ransom. That shit was hilarious." Peachy said this as the rays of the sun reflected off of his Cartier Buffs that were coated in diamonds. His large crown medallion shimmered in the sun like a bunch of glitter.

Kammron drank from his bottle of Moët with a mischievous grin on his face. "That's still the same ol' Bonkers, B. That nigga been hollering that he care about other people and whatnot, but when it came down to it, he snuffed his baby mother and his kid. Now he throwing a bitch under the bus just to live to fight another day. Dunn be wil'ing."

The big yacht swayed from side to side. The water spoke a calm language as the yacht cruised through the Ocean. It was a bright and sunny day with barely any wind. The scent was that of the sea and of Peachy's throwback Purple Haze strand that left thick clouds of smoke in the sky.

Peachy patted his lap and a gorgeous, thick Mexican woman took a seat on him. Her breasts were practically spilling out of her Burberry bikini. He kissed her on the neck. Between her globes was a small crown that was decorated in pink diamonds. "Yo, why you didn't give the order for me to drill that nigga? I had him dead to rights - him and the bitch that slugged you up. What gives?"

Kammron laughed and shrugged his shoulders. "I got my reasons, and they ain't to be discussed. You already know how this shit goes."

Peachy nodded. "Yeah, I guess. But y'all do shit real different than we do over in Queens, or how my mans do shit in the Boogie Down Bronx. It is what it is though. This puts me up one."

Kammron laughed harder. "Yeah, I figured you'd make sure that was known. I wouldn't expect no different."

"As long as you know." Peachy side-eyed Kammron as he watched three dolphins hop out of the sea, go high into the air before they came crashing down into the water again. "So why did you call this meeting, Kammron? I know how you get down. You don't usually show up in person unless it's something serious."

Kammron eyed the dolphins and drank from his bottle again. "I'm coming for Queens, Peachy."

"Yo, that's what's up. I still think it would have been easier for you to do that had you let me slump Bonkers a few days ago. That would have been one less nigga you had to worry about."

Kammron smiled and set his bottle down. He scooted to the edge of the white leather chair that he was sitting on. "N'all, kid, I don't think you're hearing me correctly. I'm set to be getting a major shipment in from the Middle East sometime next week. It's a shipment so large that Harlem won't be able to contain it. Neither will our chapters out in Brooklyn, which is why I got ground troops out that way expanding our efforts."

"Awright then, so what do you want from me?" Peachy asked this while drinking from Kammron's bottle.

This was something that Kammron found so disgusting and so disrespectful that it made him want to spit in Peachy's face. Kammron grabbed his bottle from the table and threw it into the water once Peachy had set it back on the table that was before them. "Nigga, what I'm saying is that I'm coming for all of Queens. From black to brown, white to Asian, the whole borough, and I need to know right now what that looks like for us?"

Peachy's eyes got really low. He jerked his head back when he began to comprehend just what Kammron was getting at. "Oh, muthafucka. Wait a minute. So you're saying that you're coming for my shit too? Crown Town is included in this whole thing?"

Kammron pulled a vial of liquefied heroin out of his shirt pocket, unscrewed it, and snorted the contents up each nostril, waiting for the drug to kick in. It didn't take long. Ever since the Taliban had taken over Afghanistan, the heroin came pure and fast to the United States. Kammron was locked into the Taliban, and even had a few plugs inside of Isis K. Both plugs were in competition with each other, and as long as they were, business was good.

The drug hit Kammron's nervous system like a Mack truck. He began to scratch. "When I say the whole Queens, Peachy, that's what I mean. So tell me what this looks like for our relationship?"

Peachy stood up so fast that the female sitting on his lap fell to the deck. "You snake-ass nigga! I knew I couldn't trust you. I knew I should have had the brothers get on yo' ass a long time ago. How the fuck you gon' come for my land? What type of ally does that make you?"

"I'm a Harlem American, baby. This is what we do. It's all about money for me, nigga. I don't bring emotions into this shit, and if you know what's good for you, then you wouldn't either." Kammron's eyes trailed up to Peachy's. "Now sit yo' chump ass down before we have a serious problem."

As soon as he said this, the yacht became surrounded with Harlem shooters that were on jet skis and expensive motorboats. Their fully automatic weapons were visible. Each man awaited the signal from Kammron to slay Peachy and anybody else aboard the vessel that Kammron gave the order to.

Peachy looked over the boat and cursed under his breath. He ran his fingers through his hair. "Kammron, I just got my lot solidified with the Sinaloa. I got five shipments coming in this week. I owe them six million by the end of the month and there is no negotiation around that. I can't have you steal my deck, bruh. There is no way that I can survive without going on the run. I'm asking you to stall me out."

Kammron had dozed off. He hadn't heard a single word. When he came to, he pulled his nose. "Bitch, what's it gon' be? Bow down or get prepared to go to war by tomorrow. What you wanna do?"

Peachy turned bright red. He balled his hands into fists and couldn't stop shaking. He closed his eyes for a second before he opened them and stared intently into Kammron's. What he saw was a menacing psychopath with a short fuse and no soul. This frightened him - something that nobody would ever know. "What's it gon' take to keep my end of Queens?"

"Nothing. I need it all. The only way you can even be a part of the equation is if you work under the Coke Kings, and even then, I don't like the fact that you are partially owned by the Sinaloans. I don't fuck with them clowns. They may be the only entity on earth that's more shiesty than the don." Kammron cackled at that statement.

"I'll do what it takes, Kammron. I'll make sure that me and my army handle bidness for you, and them. This won't be my first time making something like this work. I been in the Game a long time."

"Nigga, you ain't shit but thirty-three." Kammron laughed.

"Yeah, but when it comes to the Game, that's a seasoned vet. Just give me chance to show you how me and mines will get down before you get to hollering that war shit. Let that be the last result. Deal?"

Peachy really didn't want to go to war with two boroughs, and especially not Brooklyn and Harlem, which were two of the most deadly boroughs in New York. On top of that, he already knew that there was no way that he could make any money while warring, and the Sinaloa cartel was not going to play about him making his six million dollar deadline. If he needed to finesse Kammron in order to keep everything running smoothly, he knew that he would, but war was the last and stupidest option that he could not afford.

"Yo, had I never met ya crazy ass up in Riker's and you didn't have my back when the Vegas crew tried to annihilate me, I would have told you to kiss my ass right now, but you did, and I can't. I'ma let you stay on board, and we'll work out the logistics." Kammron cleared his throat and hawked a loogey over the edge of the boat. He wiped his mouth on a pink handkerchief. "However, I will say this. If ever it comes down to you getting in the way of my money or my structure, I'ma call us even and I gotta let street justice take its course. Ain't no friends in this shit. You should know that better than anybody."

Peachy nodded. "It's all good. I appreciate the play. Let's just get money and let the cards fall where they may. That's all we can really do anyway."

Kammron stood up and gave the signal. Suddenly motorboats pulled closer to the edge of the yacht and the occupants from those boats climbed aboard. In a matter of minutes, the entire yacht was saturated with sexy women and cold-blooded killers from Harlem. Kammron stood up on the white leather couch and held two bottles of Moët in the air. "This is to the new turf of Queens. We snatched Brooklyn, Harlem, and now we taking over Queens. That will be the Medina, the new Harlem, where each of our hustlers can get money until they're blue in the face. That's what Harlem niggas do, bitch. We get money. We take over decks and we get money. To Harlem!"

"To Harlem!" the crowd yelled boisterously.

Kammron stepped back down with a huge smile on his face. "This shit is only the beginning. The best is yet to come; believe that shit. Now get this nigga off my ship. This party is for Harlem only!"

Peachy felt four hands take ahold of his shirt before they tossed him into the awaiting motorboat beside the yacht. As soon as he landed, Kammron pointed in the direction of land and told him to get moving while he walked away laughing.

Peachy mugged him for a long time a little too long because the Harlem drill niggas started to aim their fullies at him one by one. He got the picture and scampered away with anger plaguing him.

Chapter 12

"Awright, it's a new day. The sun is shining, the birds woke me up this morning with their beautiful song, and today was a glorious day in church. All I gotta do is take it one minute at a time and everything will be fine. I'm speaking it into existence." Reyanna said this as she pushed her cart down the grocery aisle of Walmart.

After the huge debacle with Bonkers, all she wanted to do was get on to the next phase of things whatever that exactly was. She'd just gotten her first dose of the Pfizer vaccine and her goal was to get home and in the bed before all of the wooziness started.

She stopped in front of the produce aisle and picked up a cassava melon. She looked it over for a short time and placed it inside of her buggy. Next was the strawberry section, which was her favorite fruit. She looked the brands over carefully and picked up a few packages from her favorite vendor. Once she was done shopping for her fruits, she gathered up her spices, then her cereals, and headed to the self-checkout section of the store. She fought the urge to curse out loud when she got there. All three lanes for self-checkout where occupied with at least five waiting customers. She looked over to the aisles where there were cashiers and those lanes were even worse. She hung her head and sighed. "What is life?"

Henny stepped on the welcome mat to the store, texting away on her cell phone. Kammron just had to have collard greens, candied yams, and Jamaican jerk chicken with all of the fixings. She didn't feel like cooking. Alicia Keys was performing at the Garden tomorrow and she just had to be there, so she thought it was in her best interest to get Kammron in the best of moods today so that she wouldn't have to worry about it later. "Yo, word is bond, sometimes I hate niggas," she mumbled out loud.

As soon as Henny stepped through the door of Walmart, Reyanna caught sight of her. A sharp chill went down her spine. She released her grip from the shopping cart and turned her Gucci purse so that it covered her stomach. She dug her hand inside of it and rubbed the length of the .9 millimeter inside of it. "I should drill this bitch in front of everybody, straight up." She watched Henny disappear toward the back of the store, still texting away on her cell phone.

"Dang, can you move forward? Ain't nobody got all day to be sitting here waiting on yo' goofy ass to keep it pushing," a heavyset, light-skinned female snapped with her nineteen-year-old daughter beside her. Both women were mugging Reyanna with anger.

Reyanna sucked her teeth. "Yo, hold ya fuckin' horses, ma. Ya food ain't going nowhere, and that government shit ain't fine leave off of ya free-ass card. Governor Cuomo made sure of that shit."

"Say, love, don't be talking that dumb shit to my moms. Just keep it pushing, word up. We ain't trying to have a major situation up in these parts today." The caramel-skinned, equally heavyset daughter said this while brandishing a pocket knife.

Reyanna looked it over, and then up at her. She smirked. "Yeah, shorty, I see how you living. If that's ya best bet, I'ma move on. Y'all ain't about to ruin my day. God bless both of you bitches."

"BITCHES? Who the fuck you callin' a bitch?" the mother asked, pulling her cheap weave braids out of her face.

Reyanna ignored her. She began to check her items out one at a time. While she did so, she paid attention to the mirrors, trying to locate Henny again. Somehow she had disappeared from her vantage point.

After she finished bagging up her groceries, she loaded them back into the cart and began to push them outside. She was close to the front of the store when she noticed that the daughter was following her, cracking her knuckles. Reyanna stopped once she got halfway to her Bentley truck in the parking lot. "Yo, what the fuck you capping all of these antics off at me for, shorty, what you feeling?"

"Bitch, you're about to see real good. You can bet yo' bottom dollar on that shit right there." The daughter jogged away and stopped at a small purple Neon. She popped the trunk and took out two pair of brass knuckles just as her mother came pushing their cart out of the store. "Mama I got 'em. That bitch right there too." She pointed at Reyanna.

The mother rolled the cart to her daughter and allowed for her to load up the car with the groceries. She pulled her braids back into a ponytail and wrapped it into a big ball. "Say, Miss Lady, let me holler at you for a minute." The sun caused the side of the heavyset woman's face to sweat. You could see her nipples as clear as day through the shirt as the material was two sizes too small. The bottom folds of her stomach were easily displayed with each step that she took.

Reyanna loaded up the truck and closed the hatch. She stood her ground. "What it do, Queen? What you wanna holler at me about?"

The mother caught up to her with her eyes bucked. Adrenaline began to course through her steadily. "You was capping off a lot back there in the store. How you wanna handle this shit right now?"

Reyanna laughed. "Look, Miss Lady, you gotta be old enough to be my moms. I ain't tryna go there wit' you. I didn't mean no disrespect back there. How about we all just go our separate ways?"

The daughter caught up, skipping ready for action. "Nah, bitch, you disrespected my mother, and don't nobody do that and get away with it, so now you gotta answer for ya sins. Let's handle this the Red Hook way. Pull over on Claremont real quick so we can handle dis bidness."

"Li'l girl, I ain't got no time to be screwing wit' you. I got better thangs to do." Reyanna turned her back to her and got ready to step up into her truck.

The mother took a bottle of lemon juice and threw it at Reyanna's windshield as hard as she could, shattering the glass, but failing to knock it inward. "Bitch, you gon' fight today!" She backed up and got into her Neon. She allowed for her daughter to get inside of it before she slowly pulled out of the parking lot.

"Bitch, we on Claremont!" the daughter hollered.

Reyanna was so stunned by what he taken place that she couldn't move at first. Her eyes were bucked open so far that it hurt when she finally blinked. Sue thought about pulling the gun out of her purse and shooting until she was sure that she had killed both of them, but a couple of glances to her right and left told her that they were under heavy surveillance. Instead of doing that, she hopped into her truck and sped out of the lot with the driver's door still open. She got to Claremont before the pair of family members did and hopped out of her whip. Her long curly hair was already pulled into a ponytail.

The mother and daughter duo jumped out of the Neon with their brass knuckles on, ready for war. The daughter didn't waste any time. "Bitch, let's get it!" She ran full speed at Reyanna and jumped up, coming down with her fists swinging wildly.

Reyanna caught three hits to the top of her head that dazed her. She fell against the truck and tried to collect herself, but not before the big girl could rain down five more punches on her that hurt so bad she had to run a few feet to get away.

"Nah-un, bitch! Where that ass going?" The mama came out of the car and tackled her into the Neon. Now both women were jumping Reyanna.

"Get her ass, Mama. Whoop that bitch! Move a li'l bit, let me get some of that ass!" the daughter yelled before she punched Reyanna in the back of the head and jumped on her back. Now they both took to kicking and stomping her.

Reyanna curled into a ball. She hated herself for leaving the gun inside of the truck. Had she been with it, she would have murdered both women in cold blood with no hesitation.

Suddenly the mother screamed. Henny raised the two by four with the rusted nail inside of it over her head and brought it down again inside of the lady's back. This time she allowed for it to stay planted for a spell before she pulled it out dripping with blood. "Bitch, this Harlem! I don't know what y'all thought this was!"

The mother fell to her knees and screamed bloody murder. Henny kicked her in the bloody back. The mother fell to her, stomach wallowing in pain.

"Bitch, you better get yo' punk ass off of my mama!" The daughter made an effort to rush Henny.

Reyanna tripped her from the ground. She jumped up with the quickness and hopped on the daughter's back, wrapping her arm around her neck, choking her out with all of her strength, determined to kill her.

"Die, bitch! Die! I'm tired of you hoes always playing wit' me cause I'm pretty. This ain't that, trust and believe that." She squeezed harder and harder, twisting her arms to cause more pain.

Henny stomped the mother out so bad that the lady was throwing up blood. She pulled her .380 pistol out on her and aimed at her forehead. "Bitch, I ought to kill yo' ass dead, word is bond."

The mother grabbed her stomach and staggered. "This ain't have nothing to do with you. I don't even know who you is. You got yo' nose in other people bidness. Leave us alone!"

Reyanna felt the daughter go slack. She came to her knees, took the daughter's face, and slammed it so hard into the concrete seven times that it caused her skull to cave in. She wound up face first in a puddle of blood, struggling to get up.

Henny cocked her .380. "We gotta kill these bitches and get rid of their bodies. Ain't no way I'm going to jail for no shit like this. Not right now during Covid. Riker's is fucked all the way up and nasty." Henny locked eyes with Reyanna. "What do you say huh?" She looked around Claremont, which was a deserted block full of construction. Luckily for them, the crews were off on the weekends and the block was deserted.

"Smoke that bitch, then, and I'll finish this one. Matter fact…" She ran over and picked up a huge brick. She carried it over and slammed it with all of her might into the back of the daughter's head, killing her on contact.

"Noooooo!" the mother began.

Henny finished screwing in the silencer. She aimed and fired four fatal shots that left the mother's brains all over the rocky road.

It took them five minutes to get both bodies loaded into Henny's trapper, and another two minutes to flee the scene.

Thirty minutes later, the bodies were burned inside of a funeral home's incinerator that Henny had ties to inside of Harlem.

T.J. Edwards

Chapter 13

"So what made you help me back there? The last time I saw you, bullets was flying from ya gun and you were trying to take me out of the game, ma." Reyanna said this as she lit the last candle in the hotel room. Jhenè Aiko serenaded the room with her soft melodious flow, and both girls were freshly showered and chilling in Burberry robes with glasses of Pinot in their hands.

Henny licked the blunt over before she set fire to it. As soon as the smoke was in the air, she felt breezy and cool. "Yo, I guess some things might have changed."

Reyanna waited for more from her, and when there wasn't any, she sat on the couch and crossed her thick thighs. "What gives, Henny?"

Henny laughed and shrugged her shoulders again. She puffed on the blunt and then passed it over to Reyanna. As soon as Reyanna had it in her fingers, Henny stood up and started to pace. She ran her fingers through her hair and sighed.

"Yo, I know what that sighing is about right there. I know what that face is too. That's that nigga Kammron, ain't it?" Reyanna asked after only taking a few hits off of the weed.

Henny stopped mid pace and turned around to look her over. "Girl is it that obvious?"

"Only if a woman is going through the same thing with his right-hand man. Damn, girl, really though? How bad is it, I mean, considering that you're pregnant and all of that?"

Henny placed he left hand in her stomach and closed her eyes. "What did Kammron say to you when he first found out that you were pregnant with his kid? Can you remember?"

Reyanna shook her head. "Not really, because that was the night that all of that stuff kicked off between the three of us.

Remember I was ready to go tell him and you broke that shit up? One thing led to another and the next thing I knew we were having a shootout." Now that Reyanna thought about it, she felt as if she had been deprived of the elation that most women got when revealing to their man that they were carrying his seed. A slight source of anger crept into her toward Henny. She shook it off. "I mean, I'm pretty sure that he was happy to hear about that from you 'cause y'all have always been pretty tight. Right?"

She scoffed, "That nigga Kammron is stupid cocky about everything. That nigga was on his deathbed, Queen. They said that he'd lost so much blood that they had to give him a blood transfusion and if they hadn't, he would have lost his life." She turned around to face Reyanna. "Well, do you know that when he finally came to and the doctor told him that he was lucky to be alive because he survived when there was only a two percent chance that he would, that he told the doctor that he healed himself, and that a real nigga could never die from the slugs of a bitch?"

"Really?" Reyanna was stunned.

"Yeah, really. But you have to remember who we're dealing with. Kammron has always had an ego problem ever since I met him. I just didn't know that it would ever get this bad." She slumped down on the couch, weary.

Reyanna rubbed her shoulders. "Yo, you still didn't tell me what he said when you revealed that you were pregnant. I mean, it is his kid, right?"

Henny mugged her. "Yes. Who else is Killa going to let come near me?" She lowered her head. "Shoot, the only other nigga I'm even able to have contact with is Duke Da God, and he so far up those young hoes' asses that he wouldn't even think about fuckin' around with me. Not saying that I would anyway. But you feel where I'm going with this, right?"

"Yeah, I do." Reyanna continued to rub her shoulders. "Okay, so what did he say that has you feeling so out of it?"

"Kammron just made me feel like I should have been thankful to be carrying his seed. That I been thirsty all along to get pregnant by him, and that I was lucky. I don't feel any of that. I feel emotional, vulnerable, constantly irritated, and over it. I am thankful that I have my child growing inside of me, but I can't help but to feel angry by it at the same time. That nigga got money and all of that, but he seems like he will be a toxic-ass baby father. I don't know if I can deal with his ass for the rest of my life. I just don't." She covered her face with her hands and hunched over.

"Him and Bonkers ain't nothing but two of a kind. I don't know what would possess me to run away from Kammron straight to his old right-hand man. It's like I'm still with Killa, other than sometimes Bonkers have those emotional bouts where he can come up to my level, but for the most part he is just as toxic. Would you believe that he almost hung me out to dry just to escape some shit that we stumbled into over in Crown Town?"

Henny picked her head up and nodded. "Yeah, I can see that. In fact, I was right there in the room when Kammron gave the order for Peachy and his crew of Kings to release y'all. Had he told them to murder you two, y'all would have been left in the basement."

"Wait a minute, Killa is the one that told them to let us go?" Reyanna was fully alert now.

"Yeah, why, what's the matter?"

"I'm just not understanding why he would do that. Did the shots that he took fuck him up so bad that he didn't know that I was the one that pulled the trigger or somethin"

"N'all, he knew it was you. And he knew that he could have killed both you and Bonkers, but I guess it would have been too easy and he don't want it like that. I told you that nigga done got super cocky, more than usual."

Reyanna was quiet for a time, then she looked into Henny's eyes. "Okay, so now that brings me back to you. Why would you come to my rescue? Why not just let those hoes do me in? You catch me hobbled and finish me off? I'm sure Kammron would have a whole lot to say about you killing the female that tried to kill him, not to mention the streets as a whole. Your name would have been ringing all through New York."

"Yeah, that sounds good, but stupid. I'm on something bigger and better than a little clout." She stood up again and looked down on Reyanna. "What if I told you what there was a way for us to be filthy rich? I'm talking stupid caked up, with money on the streets and in the banks, offshore and all of that?"

"I'd say I'm listening." Reyanna stared at her more intently.

Henny looked off into space. "I ain't trying to have to have that nigga in the picture when my baby gets here. I don't want her or him born into the lifestyle that Kammron comes along with. I gotta take things into my own hands, and in doing so, secure my child's future by any means."

"So what are you saying, Queen?"

"Every move that Kammron makes, I am right there beside him like his little lap dog. He sees me as stability, and as a person that he can constantly stunt to on a regular basis. For what reason, I have no idea. However, that sort of places me within a powerful position because not only am I more often than not present, I am also in charge of Kammron's finances. I make sure that the numbers add up, and I have the knowledge of all of his codes and passwords because he forgets them all day every day." She stopped and started to nod her head.

"Girl, so what are you saying, that we kill him or something?" Reyanna didn't mind. She didn't care that he was her child's father. She was sure that sooner or later, Kammron was going to enact his revenge on her whether she was his baby mother or not, so it was best that she got down on him first.

Henny waved her off. "Killing him is too easy. Right now anyway. The first thing we need to do is to strip him of his resources from the inside out. Then we'll come for his street money, then his power, and then we'll dead his ass. What's crazy is that we have to get a move on though because that fool just been given the green light to take over Queens by Flocka, and Flocka has also given him the go ahead to take out Bonkers for whatever reason. If he kills Bonkers and takes over Queens, we're damn near through because then he will become too powerful. Those Jamaican girls all going to be all up his ass and you already know how females get down when it comes to protecting their King."

"Yeah, that means that shit would get ugly fast." Reyanna grew silent.

"Are you with me on all of this, or am I throwing too much at you all at one time?"

"N'all, you're good. I guess I'm just wondering how we went from enemies to coming together to make this happen like this? Like why are you choosing me and not some other random chick that you don't have to worry about coming in your back door and snaking you?"

Henny knelt in front of her. "Because you and I ain't never had a problem with each other if it didn't involve Kammron. The only reason that we were beefing is because of this man. We're family, girl, and I've always had mad love for you. I just couldn't see past the emotional attachment that I had to Kammron." She rubbed the side of Reyanna's face and looked into her eyes. She smiled. "Shid, I ain't gon' lie. I think one of the major reasons that I did have a problem with you when you were around Kammron is because of how beautiful I always thought you were. I mean damn, girl, where are your imperfections?"

"Yeah right," Reyanna knocked her hand away playfully.

"I'm for real." She knelt and came eye level with Reyanna. "You already know that you're killing shit. I don't even know why you're faking the funk." She held the side of her face and leaned in, kissing her lips ever so softly.

Reyanna closed her eyes and allowed for it to happen. It had been months since she'd felt any ounce of pure affection without aggression. She opened her mouth and moaned. Before she knew what was happening, both girls were locked into a passionate make out session that had both of them panting and moaning into each other's mouths.

Reyanna pushed Henny to the carpet and straddled her, kissing all over her neck. Henny grabbed ahold of Reyanna's plump backside and squeezed the globes. She pulled the flesh apart to expose the thin strip of cloth in between. The G-string separated her pussy lips. Henny pulled it to the side and searched for her crease, sliding her finger up and down the slippery slit.

Reyanna moaned at the feeling of the intrusion. She threw her head back and popped backward to try and impale herself onto Henny's finger. Henny flipped her over and laid beside her. She opened Reyanna's thighs and rubbed all over her pussy, opening it up and admiring the shimmer of her pink. She leaned over and sniffed her box, sticking her nose deep into the hole to complete the task.

"Unnn, what are you doing, Queen?" Reyanna moaned and squeezed her own titties.

Henny shivered. "Something I been wanting to do for a long time. Lay back shorty, I got this." Henny climbed between her thighs and pushed her knees to her armpits, bussing her pussy wide open. She covered her entire gap with her mouth, sucking he juices, while her tongue ran up and down the slit wildly.

Reyanna bucked and sat upright before falling back down to the carpet. She felt Henny circling her clitoris that hadn't been touched in months and the sensation caused her to scream out and cum with an ear-piercing scream. She locked her ankles around Henny's head and twitched on the carpet until the feeling left her jerking like crazy.

Henny moved from between her legs sucking her fingers one by one. She smiled down on Reyanna. "Yeah, I can see that I'm going to enjoy having you as my right hand. I been wanting to taste what that Spanish chocolate be like for a long time, and I gotta say that I am not disappointed." She sucked her fingers again for good measure.

Reyanna was still shaking. She came to her knees and took ahold of Henny. She tongued her down loudly, groaning into her mouth. "Okay, I'm 'bout what you 'bout, but we gotta be smart with this shit. I don't honestly know what you got up your sleeve, but I'ma play my role. That's all I can do." She kissed her again and stood up on weak legs, still not believing the level of climax that Henny had brought to her in such little time.

Henny stood and held Reyanna's face in both hands. "Just let me run the show, and I promise you I'ma make sure that us Queens leave out on top. Ain't nothing like the power of pussy anyway. Ain't that right?" She slipped two fingers back up Reyanna from behind, slowly working them in and out.

Reyanna closed her eyes in ecstasy. "Right."

T.J. Edwards

Chapter 14

Bonkers stood in the middle of the warehouse, stroking the sparse hairs of his chin while he watched twenty of his men and women perform their tasks according to his will. On the one side of the old warehouse were twelve women with all-black masks covering half of their faces. They sat naked and were chopping through kilo after kilo of pure South Korean heroin before they weighed and packaged it up in bundles of four and a half ounces at a time.

On the other side of the room, Bonkers had the men just as naked. They packaged large quantities of crystal methamphetamine that was so pure it had a stench that made the average person choke even from across the room. The operation seemed to run smoothly. One side of the table would chop up, separate, and weigh the product, while the workers on the other sides of the long tables would bag and drop the product into the delivery bags for certain portions of Queens and Staten Island, a new region that Bonkers was now trying desperately to invade.

Bonkers took a deep breath and kept looking over the face of his phone, hoping that it would ring. He had a major kingpin to connect with and as long as he was able to convince him to see things his way, his life in the Game would add no less than ten years to it, and at least fifty million. But if he couldn't, things were about turn bloodier than a horror movie. Either way, he had to be prepared.

***

Kammron rubbed his nose and barely opened his eyes enough to tie the Gucci belt around his left arm. He pulled it with his teeth before he grabbed the juiced-up syringe off of his dresser and sank the needle into his vein, injecting the heroin into his system. His eyes rolled into the back of his head. "Aww fuck, that's the shit right there, Fleet." He licked his lips and removed the syringe.

Flocka rubbed his hands together and nodded as he sat across the table from Kammron inside of Miss Janky's diner. It had been quite the task for Flocka when it came to finding a strategic way into the country that would allow him to evade the authorities as well as his opps, but as usual, at the end of the day, money talks, and bullshit was connected to broke niggas. They had already had a four course Jamaican dinner and both men were full and seemingly ready to explode. "I told you, mon, me tink dat da sole coming out of Africa is much stronger don dee Asian stuff. Whatta ya tink?"

Kammron was too busy inside of a nod that had him drooling at the mouth. It took him a full two minutes to come back too. He wiped his mouth and closed his eyes. "Yo, word is bond, Jamrock, I don't know what the fuck that shit is right there, but that shit got me on a whole other planet. Fuck, you finna rock wit' me for a birdie apiece?"

Flocka slammed his hand on the table laughing at the top of his lungs. "Days what me like to hear. Out dare I got a thousand of dese kilos in the semi-truck. Shipment just came from my plug from dee motherland. I'll front you the truck and you pay me fifty million. We can call it square, how 'bout dat?"

Kammron rubbed his nose. "Fifty million, huh. I give you fifty million and a thousand of these muthafuckas come to me just like that?"

Flocka nodded. 'They are already out front." As soon as he said this, a banana truck pulled out front and stepped on its air brakes. Flocka pointed. "Dat dare is my man. We grew up together. We was poor together and now we are getting rich together. That's supposed to be the way that the game goes.

I'll introduce you because from here on out he'll be your contact. I got business in Europe." Flocka stood up and waited for his right-hand man to jump out of the truck. When Duke Da God jumped out of it, Flocka stood confused. "What? How is he up dare. Where is Yul?"

Kammron laughed and upped two gold .44 Desert Eagles. "Bitch, you should have already known it was just a matter of time before I came for everything that is owed to me. I don't bow down or do bidness wit' no kings. I am the only one fit to be king." He cocked his hammers.

Flocka's eyes got big, and then they lowered. He smiled and looked around at how the Jamaicans in the restaurant that were once standing behind him on security where now on the other side of the room blended in with the Coke Kings. They had nasty mugs on their faces and eyed him as if he were their mortal enemy.

"Yeah, nigga, you see, I'ma fully invested in Jamaica, starting with the slums of Kingston. I'ma feed the starving and make sure that they ain't never gotta worry about shit ever again. I'ma make sure that the mothers of Jamaica are always taken care of on every level, and most importantly, the god is going to bring the new Harlem to Jamaica. We are going to be one, just the way that the man above intended. With all that said, and after hearing how you ain't never done shit but flaunt your wealth and flexed on your people, it seems like they were looking for the much needed change in leadership. So, bitch, you got any last words? Words for the people that you publically shitted on?"

Flocka sat down and grabbed the bottle of Hennessey. He laughed and shook his head. His took the Gucci rubber band out of his dreads and allowed for them to fall all over his face. He started to guzzle the bottle as if he were dying of thirst.

Then he slammed the bottle on the table. "Do it ya bombaclot gorilla! Do it now!"

"N'all, bitch, it ain't for me to do. Y'all want a new revolution, then waste his punk ass and welcome yourselves into the new Harlem." Kammron stepped to the side.

As soon as he did, the Jamaicans pulled out their machetes and attacked Flocka with a murderous intent. Flocka hollered as one blade after the next slammed into his face again and again. He tried to fight off his attackers, to no avail. In a matter of ten minutes, pieces of him were all over the dining room. Blood littered the floor, and the citizens of new Harlem rejoiced, barefoot dancing on his soul.

Kammron placed his arm around Duke Da God's shoulders. "Nigga, this just opened a whole new avenue for us. I told you as long as I'm running shit, we'd be straight. Take that truck to the safe house and unload it. After you through with that, I got some other shit I need you to handle. Hurry up, my nigga, time is muthafuckin' money." He popped Duke on the back of the head and walked off.

Duke Da God stood there for a moment watching Kammron get inside of his brand-new cherry red Aston Martin. The Jamaicans that had just taken part in the slaying of Flocka were now loading up in cherry BMWs and following behind Kammron to cement the fact that he was being seen as their new king.

The entire time Duke had been a part of Kammron's operation, he had never understood how someone so arrogant could ever have so much convinciblity. But it seemed like no matter what new turf Kammron wanted to take over, he never seemed to have a problem doing exactly that. Duke could still feel the smack stinging the back of his head. He laughed and walked away. "Yeah, awright, Killa, I got you, Dunn."

Chapter 15

Kammron walked circles around the slightly pudgy, caramel-skinned man three times while he himself puffed on a Cuban cigar stuffed with Exotic. He couldn't help shaking his head. "Yo, kid, so you telling me that this nigga is supposed to look like me? That's how far you think the god has fallen?"

Khabir took his small silk towel and wiped off his three carat diamond ring. "Once again, Kammron, when you get this far up in the rankings, you have to release your ego and surrender it to your brain. Intelligence is key."

"Yeah, Ock, I hear you and all that, but I'm flipping. This nigga don't look nothing like the god. He all out of shape and shit." Kammron mugged the man that was more of his doppelganger than he wanted to admit. Sipping Codeine all day long and popping Percocets had gotten him sloppy. Not only was the man identical to him, but when it came to him walking across the room, he had Kammron's swag down to the maximum. "Yo, Dunn, let me see ya stride again."

The man looked over at Khabir. Khabir nodded his head. The man got up and pranced across the floor, stepping identically to Killa. He took a seat and laid back on the couch. Khabir had fitted him in the best of pink Chanel.

"Yo, y'all wil'ing, but I guess. What's the purpose of this shit anyway?" Kammron asked Khabir.

Khabir stood in the grand living room side of the huge mansion and stretched his arms over his head. "Before I answer that question, I want to show you something that nobody else knows or has ever seen outside of this compound." He clapped his hands together loudly three times and stepped back. As soon as he did, ten identical doppelgangers came out of the back of the palace and stood behind him. They were dressed in Versace just as he was. Their hair was the same as well. You could not tell them apart unless you were alerted to the situation of what was taking place.

Khabir fanned them away and they disappeared. "You see, Kammron, I am too important of a man to risk losing my life. Therefore, I have a bunch of men that take upon my likeness that will be targeted in sacrifice for me. When they are hired, they understand the risk and they come to the conclusion fast that the reward is far greater." A baby white tiger came out of the loop area and brushed against Khabir's left leg.

Kammron made the man stand up again while he rubbed his chin. "Aw, so now I see what you're saying. That shit makes all of the sense in the world." He walked around the man again. "Yo, you understand where my Arab man's coming from wit' all of dis?"

The man nodded. "I do."

Kammron looked him over closely. "So you get that the god got all types of enemies that's coming at me on a daily that in any second you could be taken out by one of them thinking that you are me?"

"I understand one hundred percent and in honor of Khabir, I am ready and willing to be sacrificed as long as it means that my family will live good from my dying day on back, and that while I am here on earth, I will live as good as you live. Can you grant me that?"

Kammron jerked his head back. "Nigga, hell n'all. I'm Killa muthafuckin' Kam. Can't nobody live the life I live but me. Khabir, what is this fool talking about?"

Khabir held up his hand. "I'll take care of it. In the meantime, humble yourself. With a crown comes wisdom, which you seem to not have taken to. That worries me."

"Nah, kid, don't worry about me. Worry about any muthafucka that thank I'm stupid enough to not put they ass down if they violate the god, word up." He walked over to his doppelganger. "Yo, I gotta get some more of you niggas. Who else in yo' family look just like you do?"

***

It was a dark and stormy night in Camden, New Jersey when Bonkers pulled his Seven Series into the Peter McGuire Housing Projects and was ushered into the back of the deadly high rise by a team of street war veterans. Thy walked alongside of his car with assault rifles in their hands and red ski masks covering their faces. When he made it to the destination that they led him to, he was made to get out. They placed a black pillowcase over his head and led him up flights of stairs that smelled like piss, feces, and dead animals. Then they took him into an apartment with a long table. He was made to sit. All of the gunmen stepped out of the room and Bonkers couldn't hear anything other than whispering. Ten minutes later, the pillowcase was snatched off of his head and he came face to face with Duke Da God. His eyes grew as big as pool balls.

Duke Da God smiled sinisterly. "Nigga, I guess the look on yo' face ain't doing shit but telling me that you ain't done yo' homework on who the connect was supposed to be on the other side of the George Washington's Bridge, huh, nigga."

Bonkers thought about going for the .40 Glock on his waist. He should have known better than to trust a middle man from Queens. Somehow things always led back to Kammron. "Awright, nigga, you got me. You got me caught up in a sticky. So what are you going to do?"

Duke Da God sat at the head of the table. He clasped his fingers together and looked calm and cool. "This ain't no murder mission, homie. If it was, I would have never wasted my time allowing you to get this far upstairs. You saw that army of cutthroats downstairs, didn't you?"

Bonkers nodded. "Yeah, I saw them."

"Yeah, well, those muthafuckas down there run under me. Those are the drill niggas that's going crazy for the god on this Woo shit. Woo shit that I stand at the top of. You understanding that, Bonkers?"

Bonkers laughed. "Yeah bruh. So what, you lure me out here saying that you had that ninety-eight percent dog food for the low, only so you could show me what type of operation you're running? Or are you really holding like you say you is?"

Duke sat still for a moment. Then he slammed his hand on the table three times. "Let's go!"

Henny appeared from the back with a duffle bag over her shoulder. She refused to even glance Bonkers's way. She set the bag on the table and unzipped it. She reached inside and pulled out a kilo of Saudi Arabian heroin. There was Arabic written all over the package warning the handler that the product was extremely potent and dangerous. She took a pocket knife and sliced a small portion of it and took a blade full of heroin out of it. She handed it over to Bonkers for him to appraise.

Bonkers looked it over in amazement. He'd been dealing heroin his whole life. He knew a potent product when he saw it, and what he had before him was most definitely that. Not only was it potent to the eye, but it stank terribly. "So what are you sayin', Duke? You tryna fuck wit' me on this hustle shit a somethin'?"

"That depends, my nigga."

"Depends on what? What that nigga Kammron gotta say of he's still alive? That it?"

Henny mugged him. "Hell yeah, Kammron is alive. You already know that he don't die for nobody."

Bonkers scoffed, "Why am I here, Duke? Tell me what you got up your sleeve or else we ain't doing shit but flirting."

Duke kept his eyes pinned on him. "A merger. Queens is the new borough in New York that Kammron is coming for. There is a lot of development with the city that's about to take place there within the next five years and before that goes into effect, there is going to be a major form of gentrification. They are going to allow for the crime rate to rise as high as it can, and the police response time in the borough will be purposely delayed. On top of that, the flood gates for narcotics will be allowed. In three years times, an easy five hundred million in sales will be possible, but it will only be possible for one mob, and Kammron wants to make sure that the Coke Kings are that mob. He is headed by the Royal Arab Khabir and now the Jamaicans. There is no doubt in my mind that if he is able to fully take over Queens, that all of us are going to be obsolete in the grand scheme of things."

"So what you saying? That we come together to oust the nigga?" He was in disbelief. He looked over at Henny. "Ain't she pregnant? I'm looking at her belly right now and she seem like she pregnant as hell."

"Don't worry about my state, Bonkers. What I got going on inside of me ain't got shit to do with you," Henny snapped.

"Bonkers, I ain't never had nothing against you, B. All of that heat and shit that you and Killa had going on was some other shit. I mean, I always thought kid was wild for fuckin' wit' ya woman and all of that, but I couldn't really say shit seeing as I wound up getting his baby mama pregnant - you know, before she got kilt and all of that. But that's another story. Anyway, I wanna fuck wit' you. I'ma need yo' army and a few of ya connects that get down wit' those blikkas. We can't let Kammron rise like this. Shit about to get real serious real fast if we do," Duke said while frowning.

"And you down wit' this shit too, Henny?"

"N'all, Bonkers, that's why I'm standing right here ironed the fuck up, 'cause I ain't down with what's about to pop off." She rolled her eyes. "Of course I am. That nigga Kammron is nuts. He don't care about nobody but himself. We gotta get 'em while the getting is good. That's real talk."

Bonkers nodded and drifted off in thought for a moment before he snapped out of it. He extended his hand to Duke Da God. "Awright, den, once we knock kid off, I guess me and you will figure out how were going to break up New York so that each of our crews are eating the way they supposed too, right?"

Duke tightened his grip. "That's all I care about, although I ain't so much feeling New York no more. The god got major shit kicking over here in Jersey. I like my set-up. This might be one of my many duck offs. But that ain't important right now. Let's get our ducks in a row so we can make shit happen. It's all love to the gods, word up." He gave Bonkers a half of hug.

Henny eyed both men carefully with major adrenaline running through her. She stepped up to Bonkers and held out her arms. "I know shit always been estranged between us, but it's all love and war, big homie. I'm loyal to those who loyal to me. But don't bring up my pregnancy situation again. That make me feel like you're trying to say I got a weakness for a man that don't give a fuck about nobody when I'd never be one of those bimbo type of females. Hug it out, Slime."

Bonkers hugged her and took a step back, eyeing her beautiful face. "Yo, I don't know what Killa did to you to make you switch sides. I mean, I can only imagine. But all you need to know is that I ain't gon' ever cross you. As long as we working on the same team, you will have my devoted loyalty, one hunnit percent. Cool?"

Henny nodded. "It's all love and war Bonkers. We good."

"Then it's set then. For the next week, all three of us will get shit set in place so that we can annihilate Kammron. The king of Harlem is finally about to go down, and I already know the entire east coast can't wait for that." Duke slapped his hands together and proceeded to rub them anxiously.

Henny lowered her eyes. "Yeah, it's about to be a brand-new day."

Bonkers nodded. "It's long overdue. Let's get to it, word up."

T.J. Edwards

Chapter 16

"Yo, Nick, you know I don't even be coming to see niggas in the pen. The fact that I'm all the way out here sitting in front of you should let you know that I got mad respect for the Harlem gods that came before me." Kammron said this before he picked up the pineapple soda pop and twisted the cap.

Nicky Barnes sat across from him in the small gray chair inside of the federal prison's visiting room. There were two little kids visiting another convict that had been arguing and fighting each other the entire time. Nicky watched the little white boy chase his four-year-old sister around the chairs with a green booger on his finger. The little boy was laughing so hard that he couldn't catch her.

Kammron saw this and frowned. "Yo, B, tell ya kids to hold that shit down while I'm hollering at my mans right here. Word up, we talking some real shit."

The heavyset white man with tattoos all over his face thought about giving Kammron a piece of his mind, but then he locked eyes with Nicky Barnes, the Harlem legend, and decided against it. He knew that Nicky could make things extremely dangerous for him on the inside, and for his family on the outside. He grabbed both kids and hugged them to his chest. The little boy wound up eating the booger.

Nicky looked across at Kammron. "Yo, you should know that everything that takes place out there gets back to me in here. The streets been barking about ya leadership, god, and they ain't been sending the kind of messages that make me proud. All I'm hearing about is a lot of showboating, money flashing, bodies dropping, turf taking, angry king type shit. Thy say that the borough is going under. That makes me nervous."

"What the fuck are you talking about? Better yet, who the fuck have you been talking to? 'Cause ain't none of that shit accurate." Kammron felt himself becoming hot.

"Calm down. You see, that's the problem. When you reach a boss status like you have reached, Kammron, the first thing you need to get in tune with is your emotions. If not, it is the one weakness that will cripple you."

"Yo, my emotions are in check, Dunn. Like I said, I don't know who the fuck feeding you this garbage or whatnot, but let me just allow for you to see things from my point of view. I took a borough like Harlem - the same borough that you left behind that was poor, roach and rat infested with a bunch of abandoned buildings and boarded-up houses, and turned that bitch into the black heaven that it is today. I got the average ma'fucka rolling through that bitch in Bentleys, Jags, Porsches, and everything foreign. Bills are getting paid for our people. Community centers are getting built and opened right away. We ran those gentrifying white folk up out of there and bought up the properties, keeping that bitch Black, and not only that, but I have established a new Harlem out in Brooklyn, and Queens is next. Every nigga that's from the borough that's locked in the bing ain't got no less than twenty thousand on they commissary, kid. We got lawyers on standby. Ma'fuckas ain't sitting more than three days in jail before Killa bail 'em out and all of that shit. So what the fuck more you want from me, B? Word up. 'Cause even though you are a dope legend in the borough, nigga, you wasn't doing a quarter of the shit I was doing. Not you, Hoffa, or Rich and Nate. So miss me wit' that dumb shit."

Nicky Barnes leaned forward in his seat. "Li'l nigga, who the fuck do you think you talking to? Don't you understand who the fuck Nicky is to Harlem? You dare bring yo' monka ass down here capping off at the mouth because you seeing a few pennies? Don't you know that I will strip you faster than a hoe bitch working on Frederick Douglas Boulevard?"

Kammron scoffed. "Yo, and you really think this is still the nineties, don't you?" Kammron laughed. "Bitch, this is two thousand and twenty-one. A few months from being twenty-two. Ma'fuckas don't even remember ya ass like that. Bitch, I got yo' book published to keep you relevant and this how you come at the don?" Kammron leaned forward. "Listen, nigga, as of right now, you don't exist on the throne of power. It's all me. Fuck everybody else. We taking it there. Your legacy is cemented where it is. I won't tarnish yo' rep, but if you ever holler that tough Tony bullshit to the god again, I'ma drill you, B, that's on the borough. Now I'ma get up out of here before shit get more intense than it already is. I hollered at Alpo and the god was all on board with this billion dollar take over. He still got breath in his body because of that. Regardless what the streets label him as, that nigga still a legend and I stamp his street antics. He could never be a part of the royal family that is the Coke Kings because of that snitch shit, but we all knew what it was. Oh yeah, you should get a receipt today, I had one of the Queens drop another ten bands on ya books to give you a little comfort. You got anything nice to say before I get up out of here?"

Nicky Barnes leaned across the table into Kammron's face. "Nigga, you are the most ungrateful muthafucka that I ever met. If I was still on the streets, I would crush yo' bitch ass into pieces. You make Harlem look pussy."

Kammron's eyes grew big and then low. He sat back and busted up laughing. "Tell me how you really feel, old head. Word up. That shit is hilarious, and it's the last straw." He shook his head. "Long live Nicky Barnes, B. Nah, then again, short live yo' ass." Kammron stood up. "Yo, Nicky, it's been fun. I'll catch you in hell, my nigga. Even then, my fire gon' burn hotter than yours."

Nicky Barnes hopped up, "You better hope I never get out this bitch, Kammron, 'cause if I do…"

Kammron dusted himself off. "Nah, nigga, you never will. That's on gang." Kammron brushed his nose and winked.

"The fuck?" Nicky uttered.

Before he understand the signal that Kammron had just given, the same heavyset white man from before with the children hopped up and closed in on Nicky Barnes. He took his metal shank and slammed it into Nicky's neck four quick times, dropping Nicky to his knees. Nicky held the puncture wounds with blood leaking through his fingers. He hopped up and rushed Kammron, but before he could make it to him, the white stabber jumped on his back and proceeded to stab him over and over again with no mercy. Kammron walked out of the visiting room with a sly smile on his face. Business was business. Now the legend of Nicky could finally be put to rest and the world could focus in on the legend of Kammron.

***

Two weeks later, Kammron started to go harder than he ever had before. He moved five teams of cold-blooded drill artists into Queens with the sole mission of flat-lining every rogue Jamaican or opposition that went against his agenda. He gave the order to not even spare any women and children. If they were in the way, then they were to be out down just as well. Whenever his crew pulled a drill by the masses, he had the territory cleaned out, and then he filled it with hustlers from Harlem that ranged in ages from 13-16. Kammron felt that the younger the worker, the more loyal and dedicated they would be to him. In a matter of three weeks, Kammron saw his profit margin rise by thirty percent, and the city of New York saw its murder rate climb by eleven percent.

In a month's time, Kammron had given the order for so many murders that now the opp was starting to flee to different cities. They all heard how Kammron was coming with his team of Harlem lunatics and they wanted no parts of it. They fled to other safer grounds to get out of the way of his volatile takeover. In two months' time, Queens had been renamed the Medina of Harlem and there were more Harlem niggas and bitches there than there were Queens residents.

Kammron became filthy rich and so powerful that it was scary. Grossing three million dollars a day in Queens alone, his profit for a twenty-four hour span averaged twelve million. The more money he saw, the more drugs he couldn't help but to force into his system. If running Harlem was stressful, adding Brooklyn and Queens made things seemingly impossible. There was always somebody with their hand out, and there was always a problem that needed to be solved. As soon as he would get five things in order, six would fall out of order. He was beginning to understand that the Game wasn't what it was cracked up to be. And then things got worse.

There was a major rumor going around that Kammron was the sole King responsible for Nicky Barnes's hit, and while Nicky wasn't as relevant to Harlem as Kammron, there were a lot of old heads that had eaten off of Nicky's plate, and they felt utter disdain for Kammron. They banded together and vowed that whenever they saw the new god of Harlem, they would put take him out of the game. This posed a major threat for Kammron because when it came to the old heads, they were mixed in everywhere from the dope fiends to the black men that that ran the bodega and liquor stores in the neighborhood. Kammron had so many enemies that existing seemed impossible. To cope, he shot up more and more dope until he felt numb to it all.

Chapter 17

Henny came into the walk-up one day where she and Kammron had been staying to find Kammron sitting on the couch with a kilo of heroin in front of him, and an F&N in each hand. He had ten safes opened behind him, and on the floor was so much money that it looked unbelievable. His eyes were bucked wide open and there was sweat moving down the side of his face. She froze in her tracks and grew confused. "Killa, baby, what's going on?"

Kammron blinked repeatedly and wiped his mouth with his hand, accidentally touching the trigger of the F&N that was in his right hand and emitting a red beam from it. "Yo, I don't know if I can do this shit no more, shorty."

Henny winced. "What?"

"Bitch, you heard what I said. I don't thank I can do this shit anymore. Ain't nowhere else to go. I done went up as high as I can go. I got all of the money I will ever need. I'm making twenty million a day, but I got so many ma'fuckas to feed, and it's always something. Somebody always needs me for something. I pay everybody bills. Doctor bills, lawyer fees, bails, funerals, car, house, insurance, groceries. I do it all. All ma'fuckas see me as is a walking lick. I barely say no, but whenever I do, the world wanna go to Facebook or TikTok and talk about how I'm shitting on my people. I got niggas trying to drill me everywhere I go. I'm ducking one indictment after the next, and even though the governor gave me immunity, they indicting my niggas left and right and everybody ain't loyal. Shid, I even got the Taliban wanting to knock my head off 'cause I got heroin deals lined up until November of 2022 wit' Isis K. This shit is ridiculous. So yeah, I don't thank I can handle this shit no more. I want out."

Henny came into the living room and stood in front of him. "How does that even work, Killa? You are feeding so many people. If you walk away right now, they are going to starve, not to mention that they are going to turn their back on you and become your enemy. The one thing that you don't need is more enemies."

"Yo, I done had enemies my whole life. My daddy wanted to kill me the first day I was born because they charged him six gees for my birthing expenses. I ain't worried about no enemies, Henny. I'm over this shit!" He leaned his head forward and laid his cheek on her stomach. "I wanna be a family now. I want me and you and our baby to stroll away to California and live in the hills. I wanna start from scratch. I wanna put that diamond on ya finger and have you as my missus. You've always had the best slot. I don't need a bunch of bitches. All I need is you. It's always been you, word is bond."

Henny grew weak. Her knees began to buckle. "Really, Killa? Oh my God, daddy, I don't know what to say." She dropped down to his knees and wrapped her arms around his body. "I been crazy about you. All I've ever wanted was for us is to be a family and to get away from all of this shit out here in New York. It's time to make a change."

"I know, boo, that's what I'm saying. I say we leave under the cover of darkness and just go. We ain't gotta let nobody know shit. It can just be me and you. The world will never know what happened. What do you think?"

Tears were in Henny's eyes now. She nodded her head as she hugged him. "Yes, daddy, let's do it. Let's get the heck out of here tonight." She hugged him as tight as she could. Kammron kissed her forehead. Henny kissed his lips before she stood up and wiped away her tears. "So how do we do this?"

Kammron scratched his head with one of the guns. "We just go. That's how we do it. But first, baby, I gotta know. This money, the cars, the jewelry…none of this shit means anything to you, do it? Whether we got it or not it doesn't justify your love and loyalty to me, right?"

Henny shook her head. "I don't care about any of it, Kammron. I never have. All I care about is you. I love you with all of my heart."

"And you'll always have my back, against all odds, never choosing nothing over me?"

"Always, Killa. Fuck this world. All I see is you."

"Okay, baby. I guess that's why my heart is so cold." He hopped up and fired his gun into her shoulder, knocking her back three feet. She tripped over the coffee table.

"Ow! What the fuck?" Henny hollered.

Kammron stood over her. He grabbed her by her hair and dragged her into the back room, where two of his doppelgangers were laid out with bullet holes all over them. "You see this shit? Bitch, they thought these niggas was me. They thought they could kill a muthafuckin' don like they did these bitch-ass, never-could-be-me-ass niggas. But real niggas don't die. You can't kill what's already dead!"

He dragged her from that room into the next, where Bonkers', Duke Da God's, and Reyanna's bodies were laid on top of one another, bullet-ridden and decomposing. "This what the fuck you get when you cross Killa, bitch. You smell that shit, huh? Take a deep breath. It smell good, don't it?" He laughed and flung her on top of Reyanna. "Y'all are the reason a nigga should never trust nobody. That's why it's fuck everybody. Ya hate to see greatness, but I can't help that. I can't help none of that shit!"

"But Killa, yo' seed. At least stall me out because I'm carrying yo'–"

Kammron placed the guns to her forehead and pulled the triggers back to back to back to back to back until they were both clicking. "Rest in disloyalty, bitch, just like the rest of 'em." He dropped his guns on the floor and closed the door.

He sat back in the living room for a few moments before he drew up a hefty dose of heroin, three times as much as usual. He closed his eyes and injected the poison at the same time the front door was kicked in and the old school killas surrounded him with their revolvers already out. They released slug after slug into his body, twisting him on the couch. Kammron fell to the floor while they retreated with a pained smile on his face. He kept his eyelids open as everything faded to black.

The End

Lock Down Publications and Ca$h Presents assisted publishing packages.

BASIC PACKAGE $499
Editing
Cover Design
Formatting

UPGRADED PACKAGE $800
Typing
Editing
Cover Design
Formatting

ADVANCE PACKAGE $1,200
Typing
Editing
Cover Design
Formatting
Copyright registration
Proofreading
Upload book to Amazon

LDP SUPREME PACKAGE $1,500
Typing
Editing
Cover Design
Formatting
Copyright registration
Proofreading
Set up Amazon account
Upload book to Amazon

Advertise on LDP Amazon and Facebook page

***Other services available upon request. Additional charges may apply
Lock Down Publications
P.O. Box 944
Stockbridge, GA 30281-9998
Phone # 470 303-9761

Submission Guideline

Submit the first three chapters of your completed manuscript to ldpsubmissions@gmail.com, subject line: Your book's title. The manuscript must be in a .doc file and sent as an attachment. Document should be in Times New Roman, double spaced and in size 12 font. Also, provide your synopsis and full contact information. If sending multiple submissions, they must each be in a separate email.

Have a story but no way to send it electronically? You can still submit to LDP/Ca$h Presents. Send in the first three chapters, written or typed, of your completed manuscript to:

LDP: Submissions Dept
Po Box 944
Stockbridge, Ga 30281

DO NOT send original manuscript. Must be a duplicate.

Provide your synopsis and a cover letter containing your full contact information.

Thanks for considering LDP and Ca$h Presents.

<u>NEW RELEASES</u>

QUEEN OF THE ZOO by BLACK MIGO
MOB TIES 4 by SAYNOMORE
THE BRICK MAN by KING RIO
KINGZ OF THE GAME by PLAYA RAY
VICIOUS LOYALTY by KINGPEN
STRAIGHT BEAST MODE by DEKARI
COKE KINGS 5 by T.J. EDWARDS

Coming Soon from Lock Down Publications/Ca$h Presents
BLOOD OF A BOSS **VI**
SHADOWS OF THE GAME II
TRAP BASTARD II
By **Askari**
LOYAL TO THE GAME **IV**
By **T.J. & Jelissa**
IF TRUE SAVAGE **VIII**
MIDNIGHT CARTEL IV
DOPE BOY MAGIC IV
CITY OF KINGZ III
NIGHTMARE ON SILENT AVE II
By **Chris Green**
BLAST FOR ME **III**
A SAVAGE DOPEBOY III
CUTTHROAT MAFIA III
DUFFLE BAG CARTEL VII
HEARTLESS GOON VI
By **Ghost**
A HUSTLER'S DECEIT III
KILL ZONE II
BAE BELONGS TO ME III
By **Aryanna**
KING OF THE TRAP III
By **T.J. Edwards**
GORILLAZ IN THE BAY V
3X KRAZY III

T.J. Edwards

STRAIGHT BEAST MODE II

De'Kari

KINGPIN KILLAZ IV

STREET KINGS III

PAID IN BLOOD III

CARTEL KILLAZ IV

DOPE GODS III

Hood Rich

SINS OF A HUSTLA II

ASAD

RICH $AVAGE II

By Troublesome

YAYO V

Bred In The Game 2

S. Allen

CREAM III

By Yolanda Moore

SON OF A DOPE FIEND III

HEAVEN GOT A GHETTO II

By Renta

LOYALTY AIN'T PROMISED III

By Keith Williams

I'M NOTHING WITHOUT HIS LOVE II

SINS OF A THUG II

TO THE THUG I LOVED BEFORE II

By Monet Dragun

QUIET MONEY IV

EXTENDED CLIP III

THUG LIFE IV

By **Trai'Quan**

THE STREETS MADE ME IV

By **Larry D. Wright**

IF YOU CROSS ME ONCE II

By **Anthony Fields**

THE STREETS WILL NEVER CLOSE II

By K'ajji

HARD AND RUTHLESS III

THE BILLIONAIRE BENTLEYS II

Von Diesel

KILLA KOUNTY II

By Khufu

MONEY GAME II

By Smoove Dolla

A GANGSTA'S KARMA II

By FLAME

JACK BOYZ VERSUS DOPE BOYZ

A DOPEBOY'S DREAM III

By Romell Tukes

MURDA WAS THE CASE II

Elijah R. Freeman

THE STREETS NEVER LET GO II

By Robert Baptiste

AN UNFORESEEN LOVE III

By **Meesha**

T.J. Edwards

KING OF THE TRENCHES II
by **GHOST & TRANAY ADAMS**

MONEY MAFIA

By **Jibril Williams**

QUEEN OF THE ZOO II

By **Black Migo**

THE BRICK MAN II

By King Rio

VICIOUS LOYALTY II

By Kingpen

Available Now

RESTRAINING ORDER **I & II**

By **CA$H & Coffee**

LOVE KNOWS NO BOUNDARIES **I II & III**

By **Coffee**

RAISED AS A GOON I, II, III & IV

BRED BY THE SLUMS I, II, III

BLAST FOR ME I & II

ROTTEN TO THE CORE I II III

A BRONX TALE I, II, III

DUFFLE BAG CARTEL I II III IV V VI

HEARTLESS GOON I II III IV V

A SAVAGE DOPEBOY I II

DRUG LORDS I II III

CUTTHROAT MAFIA I II

KING OF THE TRENCHES

By **Ghost**

LAY IT DOWN **I & II**

LAST OF A DYING BREED I II

BLOOD STAINS OF A SHOTTA I & II III

By **Jamaica**

LOYAL TO THE GAME I II III

LIFE OF SIN I, II III

By **TJ & Jelissa**

BLOODY COMMAS I & II

SKI MASK CARTEL I II & III

KING OF NEW YORK I II,III IV V

RISE TO POWER I II III

COKE KINGS I II III IV V

BORN HEARTLESS I II III IV

KING OF THE TRAP I II

By **T.J. Edwards**

IF LOVING HIM IS WRONG...I & II

LOVE ME EVEN WHEN IT HURTS I II III

By **Jelissa**

WHEN THE STREETS CLAP BACK I & II III

THE HEART OF A SAVAGE I II III

MONEY MAFIA

By **Jibril Williams**

T.J. Edwards

A DISTINGUISHED THUG STOLE MY HEART I II & III

LOVE SHOULDN'T HURT I II III IV

RENEGADE BOYS I II III IV

PAID IN KARMA I II III

SAVAGE STORMS I II

AN UNFORESEEN LOVE I II

By **Meesha**

A GANGSTER'S CODE I &, II III

A GANGSTER'S SYN I II III

THE SAVAGE LIFE I II III

CHAINED TO THE STREETS I II III

BLOOD ON THE MONEY I II III

By J-Blunt

PUSH IT TO THE LIMIT

By **Bre' Hayes**

BLOOD OF A BOSS **I, II, III, IV, V**

SHADOWS OF THE GAME

TRAP BASTARD

By **Askari**

THE STREETS BLEED MURDER **I, II & III**

THE HEART OF A GANGSTA I II& III

By **Jerry Jackson**

CUM FOR ME I II III IV V VI VII

An **LDP Erotica Collaboration**

BRIDE OF A HUSTLA **I II & II**

THE FETTI GIRLS **I, II& III**

CORRUPTED BY A GANGSTA I, II III, IV

BLINDED BY HIS LOVE

THE PRICE YOU PAY FOR LOVE I, II ,III

DOPE GIRL MAGIC I II III

By **Destiny Skai**

WHEN A GOOD GIRL GOES BAD

By **Adrienne**

THE COST OF LOYALTY I II III

By Kweli

A GANGSTER'S REVENGE **I II III & IV**

THE BOSS MAN'S DAUGHTERS I II III IV V

A SAVAGE LOVE **I & II**

BAE BELONGS TO ME I II

A HUSTLER'S DECEIT I, II, III

WHAT BAD BITCHES DO I, II, III

SOUL OF A MONSTER I II III

KILL ZONE

A DOPE BOY'S QUEEN I II III

By **Aryanna**

A KINGPIN'S AMBITON

A KINGPIN'S AMBITION **II**

I MURDER FOR THE DOUGH

By **Ambitious**

TRUE SAVAGE I II III IV V VI VII

DOPE BOY MAGIC I, II, III

MIDNIGHT CARTEL I II III

CITY OF KINGZ I II

NIGHTMARE ON SILENT AVE

T.J. Edwards

By **Chris Green**

A DOPEBOY'S PRAYER

By **Eddie "Wolf" Lee**

THE KING CARTEL **I, II & III**

By **Frank Gresham**

THESE NIGGAS AIN'T LOYAL **I, II & III**

By **Nikki Tee**

GANGSTA SHYT **I II &III**

By **CATO**

THE ULTIMATE BETRAYAL

By **Phoenix**

BOSS'N UP **I , II & III**

By **Royal Nicole**

I LOVE YOU TO DEATH

By **Destiny J**

I RIDE FOR MY HITTA

I STILL RIDE FOR MY HITTA

By **Misty Holt**

LOVE & CHASIN' PAPER

By **Qay Crockett**

TO DIE IN VAIN

SINS OF A HUSTLA

By **ASAD**

BROOKLYN HUSTLAZ

By **Boogsy Morina**

BROOKLYN ON LOCK I & II

By **Sonovia**

GANGSTA CITY

By **Teddy Duke**

A DRUG KING AND HIS DIAMOND I & II III

A DOPEMAN'S RICHES

HER MAN, MINE'S TOO I, II

CASH MONEY HO'S

THE WIFEY I USED TO BE I II

By Nicole Goosby

TRAPHOUSE KING **I II & III**

KINGPIN KILLAZ I II III

STREET KINGS I II

PAID IN BLOOD **I II**

CARTEL KILLAZ I II III

DOPE GODS I II

By **Hood Rich**

LIPSTICK KILLAH **I, II, III**

CRIME OF PASSION I II & III

FRIEND OR FOE I II III

By **Mimi**

STEADY MOBBN' **I, II, III**

THE STREETS STAINED MY SOUL I II

By **Marcellus Allen**

WHO SHOT YA **I, II, III**

SON OF A DOPE FIEND I II

HEAVEN GOT A GHETTO

Renta

GORILLAZ IN THE BAY **I II III IV**

T.J. Edwards

TEARS OF A GANGSTA I II

3X KRAZY I II

STRAIGHT BEAST MODE

DE'KARI

TRIGGADALE I II III

MURDAROBER WAS THE CASE

Elijah R. Freeman

GOD BLESS THE TRAPPERS I, II, III

THESE SCANDALOUS STREETS I, II, III

FEAR MY GANGSTA I, II, III IV, V

THESE STREETS DON'T LOVE NOBODY I, II

BURY ME A G I, II, III, IV, V

A GANGSTA'S EMPIRE I, II, III, IV

THE DOPEMAN'S BODYGAURD I II

THE REALEST KILLAZ I II III

THE LAST OF THE OGS I II III

Tranay Adams

THE STREETS ARE CALLING

Duquie Wilson

MARRIED TO A BOSS I II III

By Destiny Skai & Chris Green

KINGZ OF THE GAME I II III IV V VI

Playa Ray

SLAUGHTER GANG I II III

RUTHLESS HEART I II III

By Willie Slaughter

FUK SHYT

By Blakk Diamond

DON'T F#CK WITH MY HEART I II

By Linnea

ADDICTED TO THE DRAMA I II III

IN THE ARM OF HIS BOSS II

By Jamila

YAYO I II III IV

A SHOOTER'S AMBITION I II

BRED IN THE GAME

By S. Allen

TRAP GOD I II III

RICH $AVAGE

By Troublesome

FOREVER GANGSTA

GLOCKS ON SATIN SHEETS I II

By Adrian Dulan

TOE TAGZ I II III

LEVELS TO THIS SHYT I II

By Ah'Million

KINGPIN DREAMS I II III

By Paper Boi Rari

CONFESSIONS OF A GANGSTA I II III IV

By Nicholas Lock

I'M NOTHING WITHOUT HIS LOVE

SINS OF A THUG

TO THE THUG I LOVED BEFORE

By Monet Dragun

CAUGHT UP IN THE LIFE I II III

THE STREETS NEVER LET GO

By Robert Baptiste

NEW TO THE GAME I II III

MONEY, MURDER & MEMORIES I II III

By **Malik D. Rice**

LIFE OF A SAVAGE I II III

A GANGSTA'S QUR'AN I II III

MURDA SEASON I II III

GANGLAND CARTEL I II III

CHI'RAQ GANGSTAS I II III

KILLERS ON ELM STREET I II III

JACK BOYZ N DA BRONX I II III

A DOPEBOY'S DREAM I II

By **Romell Tukes**

LOYALTY AIN'T PROMISED I II

By Keith Williams

QUIET MONEY I II III

THUG LIFE I II III

EXTENDED CLIP I II

By **Trai'Quan**

THE STREETS MADE ME I II III

By **Larry D. Wright**

THE ULTIMATE SACRIFICE I, II, III, IV, V, VI

KHADIFI

IF YOU CROSS ME ONCE

ANGEL I II

IN THE BLINK OF AN EYE
By **Anthony Fields**
THE LIFE OF A HOOD STAR
By **Ca$h & Rashia Wilson**
THE STREETS WILL NEVER CLOSE
By **K'ajji**
CREAM I II
By **Yolanda Moore**
NIGHTMARES OF A HUSTLA I II III
By **King Dream**
CONCRETE KILLA I II
VICIOUS LOYALTY
By **Kingpen**
HARD AND RUTHLESS I II
MOB TOWN 251
THE BILLIONAIRE BENTLEYS
By **Von Diesel**
GHOST MOB
Stilloan Robinson
MOB TIES I II III IV
By **SayNoMore**
BODYMORE MURDERLAND I II III
By **Delmont Player**
FOR THE LOVE OF A BOSS
By **C. D. Blue**
MOBBED UP I II III IV
THE BRICK MAN

T.J. Edwards

By King Rio

KILLA KOUNTY

By Khufu

MONEY GAME

By Smoove Dolla

A GANGSTA'S KARMA

By FLAME

KING OF THE TRENCHES II

by **GHOST & TRANAY ADAMS**

QUEEN OF THE ZOO

By **Black Migo**

BOOKS BY LDP'S CEO, CA$H

TRUST IN NO MAN

TRUST IN NO MAN 2

TRUST IN NO MAN 3

BONDED BY BLOOD

SHORTY GOT A THUG

THUGS CRY

THUGS CRY 2

THUGS CRY 3

TRUST NO BITCH

TRUST NO BITCH 2

TRUST NO BITCH 3

TIL MY CASKET DROPS

RESTRAINING ORDER

RESTRAINING ORDER 2

IN LOVE WITH A CONVICT

LIFE OF A HOOD STAR

T.J. Edwards